The God of the Jews Must Die!

Brad Keating

THE GOD OF THE JEWS MUST DIE!

I would like to express my appreciation to the following people for helping me write and publish this book: Rob Lindsted for several ideas in the story and helping in the entire publishing process. Dave Cloud, for his knowledge of editing. Claire Lynn, for her help and knowledge of writing. Chris Callan, for his artistic talents in drawing the cover. And most of all, I'd like to thank Kelly Frey-Bishop, without whom this book would not have been completed.

May the Lord be magnified and His saving grace be spread by the reading of The God of the Jews Must Die.

— Brad Keating

Preface

The story you are about to read is true ... or could be. The events told in this book are the same described in the Bible, but the feelings and thoughts of the unknown author were added to enhance the overall impact of the book. It is my desire that this story will help all Christians understand the order of events for the Tribulation period. I also hope and pray that those who do not know Jesus Christ as their personal Savior would not put this book down until they have accepted the free gift of eternal life.

I began working on this story over three years ago as I wanted to comprehend how all the events described for the Tribulation could be put together in a way that made sense. I had read many commentaries and books on prophecy, but none could answer my many questions about why or how everything fit together. With the many books and study guides I read, plus my own personal studies, I began to build a story on how someone going through the Tribulation would think and feel.

A little over a year ago, the Lord led me to more reading on the soon return of His Son, Jesus Christ. I realized just how short a period of time there was left before Jesus would be meeting us in the clouds (the highlights of that study are included at the end of this book). About the same time, I was teaching a series on prophecy at our church, and was amazed at the number of people who wanted to know more about the Tribulation. Soon afterward, the Lord brought me in contact with many Christians from all walks of life who had little knowledge of the Tribulation, but a great desire to learn more. Despite an eagerness to learn, almost all expressed their dislike of having to read the informational books that require a tremendous amount of time and thought. Remarkably, I found that people's questions concerning the order of events in prophecy, reflected ones I previously held. Because of this, I decided it was time to write this book.

Writing about prophecy in story form would enable me to hand anyone who knew nothing about the Bible or prophecy a book that all could understand and enjoy reading. As a few people became involved with me in this work, they too wanted to hand people something they could read that depicted the horrors of the Tribulation period without being bogged down by too much information. Encouraged by their comments, I decided to publish this work so that others could use it for ministry purposes as well.

With all this in mind, I want to mention several aspects of the book before you begin. First, it was written on a level so that people of all ages, educational backgrounds, and experiences could fully understand what the story is telling. I steered away from big words and vague terms that would require someone to have a dictionary alongside to understand it. Second, few names were used to limit any identification with someone now. The person's name used for the Antichrist was chosen after research for a possible European leader with bank connections. I in no way endorsing that this person is the Antichrist or will be, but for the purpose of the book, someone was needed to begin with. Third, all Scripture used for this writing is in the back of the book for your own personal study. I encourage everyone who reads this to go back over the scriptures from each chapter and study them more thoroughly (using the help of other study guides if necessary). Finally, I have yet to find two prophecy authors (or speakers) who agree on everything. Whether you agree or disagree with all of my ideas, please read this with an open heart and a spirit for which it was written: to glorify the Lord Jesus Christ and show the horrors of a world in which Satan is allowed to control.

Though no book could ever describe the torment, suffering, and pain of the coming Tribulation, I pray that everyone who reads this will be more fully awakened to the reality of what God will soon do to judge the world of sin. More importantly, I pray that if you haven't accepted Jesus Christ as your personal Savior, that you do so **before you put this book down.** Otherwise, this story may be yours!

Day One

A strange thing happened this afternoon. Millions of people around the world disappeared without a trace. They left everything behind, including the clothes they were wearing. No one knows exactly what took place.

I remember working on a project at about two p.m., when my eyes blurred from staring at the report in front of me. At least, that is what I thought it was from. As I put my pencil down to gently rub my weary eyes, several sharp screams broke the soft, elevator-music-filled air. Leaping from my desk, I rushed to the door, yanking it open. Several secretaries ran to a cubicle by the window. As I started toward the commotion, my mind raced with horrifying possibilities. A heart attack? Stroke? Accident? Dismissing my anxieties for the purpose of dealing properly with whatever emergency lay ahead, I asked the ladies that had crowded into the doorway to step aside. To my amazement, there wasn't any blood or even a body lying on the floor. I stepped into the cubicle and picked up the empty clothes crumpled on the chair. Looking down at the empty socks and shoes positioned under the desk, I asked the crowd what happened. Before anyone could answer me, a lady's voice from down the hall screamed, "Mr. Gunther is missing!"

The group of onlookers hustled to Mr. Gunther's office. Working my way to the front, I saw his suit sprawled on the chair. His secretary sat next to the desk with her head in her hands as she wept. I walked over and put my hand on her shoulder. She looked up with tear-filled eyes and asked, "How can he just disappear?"

After a few moments of silence, someone yelled, "Hey, there's a report on the radio!"

We listened as the radio was turned up for all to hear.

"... whether or not this is nationwide or even worldwide. I repeat, hundreds and maybe thousands of people have just disappeared only moments ago from across our entire listening area. We do not know whether or not this is nationwide or even worldwide, but we do know that the freeways are already jammed. One car ran off the road, jumped an embankment, and ran into an intersection causing severe injuries. Apparently, the automobile that caused the accident contains no body, just clothes left in a heap on the seat with no trace of blood. Again, hundreds and maybe thousands of...".

I turned around and walked back to my office. My mind raced for an explanation to the events of the last few minutes. Sitting down in my chair, I reached for the telephone and dialed my home phone number several times, but could not get through to my wife. Several employees came in and began discussing what had happened. The rest of the afternoon was spent listening to the radio and conversing with everyone as they passed into and out of my office.

I left work at five p.m. and arrived at my house in time for the ten o'clock news. I have never seen traffic like that in my life. There were hundreds of accidents throughout the city and county. Almost all were severe and blocked traffic on every major highway. The emergency vehicles could not come close to keeping up with all the calls. Compounding the problem, almost everyone wanted to go to the gas stations and grocery stores to stock up in case the food or oil supply had been hurt in some way. This congested the traffic at almost every corner. So even after spending three and a half hours on the freeway, it took me another hour and a half to finally reach home.

To make matters worse, my wife (who can't handle any kind of an emergency) greeted me at the door with endless chatter of all the terrible things that would happen to us. I appeased her fears by agreeing to buy out the local grocery store for all our necessities, however I was going to watch the news first. She reluctantly waited until the news went off. We then spent over two hundred dollars on food items and waited an hour in line, even though it was midnight! I guess it was worth the trouble, just to see my wife smile and give me a thankful kiss. I should be more appreciative of how she cares for me and our son.

The news reports confirmed that millions have disappeared across our nation. No one has any idea what has happened. One fact we do know: the bodies are missing with no trace as to where they went. They left behind all their clothes, and not a single drop of blood was shed from any of the victims. There seems to be no pattern to the race or nationality of the victims. They came from all different walks of life.

The president declared our nation in a state of emergency and held a special broadcast. He said, "… At this time, we have no explanation for what happened this afternoon. We have few reports from other countries and do not know the global situation. We do know that our country is missing an estimated one to five million people. Our entire military defense is on red alert and watchful for any foreign intrusion. I want to take this time to personally say we need to unite in this time of need and turn this disaster into a stepping stone for our country. We cannot fall down or become disheartened, but strengthen ourselves and use this time to draw closer to each other. I, too, have lost dear friends and colleagues, but I know if they were here, they would want us to press on. For all we know, God may have taken them to slap the rest of us in the face. He wants us to wake up and realize that the hatred, stealing, killing, and evil must come to an end. No matter what the reason for the disappearance is, we must now love and help one another to make this nation greater than ever before!…"

I was really glad to hear what the president said. I know that there is too much crime and hatred amongst us. This so-called disaster could prove to be a turning point for many people. Maybe we can learn to live in harmony with each other instead of all the bickering and envy. I've always been one who believes each and every one of us has good inside. We just need to overcome the evil with this good. I know with what the president said, our country has a chance to become really good.

The news also tried to bring out all the possibilities of the disappearance. The explanations are ranging from UFOs to a new type of nuclear weapon. No one has any explanation with proof of any kind. The big rumor comes from those who say it was predicted in the Bible. Most of the newscasts are focusing on this debate. I just turned off one that featured a minister from a large church in New York. He says that nowhere in the Bible has he found any proof of such an event. He says the book of Revelation depicts a continual progress of the church since Jesus Christ. The so-called "Rapture" is never mentioned. Plus, why do so many "Christians" still remain.? Many church leaders and congregations have not been touched by the disaster. He even had some other well-known ministers with him. They never did explain what happened.

A good number of my friends think that God did have something to do with it. They agree with the president's possible explanation that it may be God's way of slapping us in our faces to wake us up. I kind of agree with them as well. I've always believed in God and gone to church and I know that God is a God of love. He probably took a few off the earth to help us get our act together. I think it proves that there really is a God.

Of course, the atheists refute the idea of God playing a part in it. They say it was UFOs that took a group away for experiments. Aliens might have invaded the world to show their power and will use that for us to bow to their demands. A possible proof of this is that many people claimed to see a flash of light at the moment of the disaster. I remember my eyes blurring and then rubbing them just before the disappearance, but I don't recall an actual flash of light.

Another outlandish story that caught my attention came

from a group of people who claim we are stepping into a "new age." The report I listened to presented some lady who explained what her group believed. She said, "God has been trying to bring us into a new stage of development for the human race, but certain narrow-minded fanatics have hindered this process. God took them off the earth to teach them Himself, thus allowing us to reach our new potential. We now look for the Christ to teach us the way to evolve to the next step on the evolutionary ladder."

The part that really stunned me was the fact that she said her group extends around the world and has been waiting for a supernatural event like this. Their group has millions of believers who have already been teaching about this new age, predicting that fanatics were going to be removed by God! This prophecy part baffles me the most. They not only have an explanation for what happened, but also have documented proof of a supernatural event like this occurring. How could anyone know anything in advance, unless God had told them He was going to do it? The fanatic part doesn't make a whole lot of sense, but I do see the possibility.

Mr. Gunther, who disappeared from work, claimed to be a Christian. He seemed like a closed-minded Bible believer to me. He continually preached about everyone being sinners and that the only way to go to Heaven was to believe in Jesus. I grew weary of listening to him preach. Talking about God and Jesus on Sundays is one thing, but not all the time. I felt really uncomfortable around him because of it. I'm a good person and attend church, but I don't go off the deep end about it. I think God wants us to show love by being kind to each other and keeping the Ten Commandments, not just preaching all the time like he did.

However, another guy I worked with who disappeared wasn't a fanatic at all. As a matter of fact, I don't think he even went to church. He seemed like everyone else. He talked with me once about God, but he seemed nervous about it. I even invited him to come to my church sometime if he wanted, but he never came. He was a Christian just like me, not a fanatic. So why did he disappear?

Week One

The sun's first glimmer through my window on Sunday morning opened my eyes, and I jumped out of bed anticipating a good sermon on the event of last week. My wife stared in amazement as I hustled across the floor and into the shower. I quickly cleaned and rinsed my entire body. As I stepped out of the bathroom drying myself, my wife greeted me with a kiss. "I've never seen you so excited about getting up since you had tickets to the big game," she stated.

"I guess I'm excited about learning some answers on what has happened. I know church will be the best place to hear some," I replied.

My wife cooked a hearty breakfast of pancakes, eggs, fruit, and sausage for my son and me. We ate leisurely for the first time since I can remember. "Don't you like eating slowly without being rushed, hon?" she asked.

"Okay, I have to admit it's nice."

"Wouldn't it be great if every morning you woke up early and cheerful?" she continued.

"Nah, it's more fun being late and grouchy," I quipped. She laughed as I snarled and picked up the dishes.

We arrived at church about fifteen minutes early, along with many other families. The parking lot was already half full and more cars were coming in. I think a lot of other people wanted some answers besides me.

My favorite deacon greeted me at the door. "Did you hear about the pastor?" he asked.

"Don't tell me . . ."

"Yep, he disappeared, along with most of the other deacons."

"Wow! What are we going to do?" my wife asked.

"We're going to decide today at the meeting," he answered.

I sat down and looked around the room. Many of the regular families were missing. Even so, the church was filling up fast with people I hadn't seen in years, as well as new ones who had never come before. I leaned over to my wife and whispered, "There are the Patricks and Burts, but I don't see the Andrews anywhere."

Another one of the deacons walked up front and began, "Friends, I know we have all gathered to hear a message and receive some answers. However, I regret to say that our church was hit very hard by the disaster. Our pastor and family are missing, plus many of the membership. The remaining deacons and I have decided that the best solution for now is to have a quiet time of remembrance today for our friends and loved ones. We will begin looking for a replacement as pastor and call headquarters for any ideas. Please register on your way out so we can keep in contact with you on any further developments."

We then prayed silently for about five minutes and were dismissed. Of course, no one left. We all visited with one another for over an hour, discussing how the disaster affected us, along with any answers as to why it happened.

On our way home, my wife and I discussed the different people who disappeared. I finally became aware of the number of people I knew personally who had left. Quite a few of my friends from church and several neighbors were missing, including an aunt and uncle from Colorado. It seems like just about everybody had a relative or close friend disappear. Our pastor's departure is the toughest one for me. I knew him well, and we shared a lot of time together. I'll miss him.

As for the world situation, we finally received reports from all the other countries a few days after the disappearance. It seems like the United States was by far the hardest hit. We were the only major country with disappearances in our top government bodies. England, Canada, West Germany, and a few others reported government people missing, but nothing like the United States. All the other countries in the world seem to be functioning as before with few changes. We are the only country with an emergency in the governing body!

We also learned that not all countries have been hit! Again, the United States by far has the most people missing. Canada and England run a distant second and third. Other European nations plus Australia, Korea, and several others have reported thousands missing, but have had little difficulty in recovering. Russia, China, Iraq, Iran, and many other countries have reported very few missing... if any! It seems like there has been little or no disturbance in their daily routines.

While all other nations continue in just about the same manner as before, we will take months and maybe years to recover from the devastation of having millions of people disappear. We must replace key personnel throughout the government on the national, state, and local levels. Furthermore, the military chain of command has been severely disrupted and needs time to put the pieces back together to function properly. On a smaller scale, just about every individual in our country has been affected in some way from missing relatives, friends, or fellow employees. I don't know how long it will take to clean up the various problems they left behind. My work load has already doubled to make up for the managers under me who disappeared. In comparison, other countries can function with few or no major changes. Their military remains intact and most businesses continue running as before. On the world scale, we have gone from being a superpower to a confused and disorganized country with no strength to help ourselves, much less anyone else!

The odd part is that, according to the reports, very few countries have any real sympathy for us. Many countries felt we deserved punishment anyway. Third World nations have a *laissez-faire* attitude with some expression of disbelief on the whole thing. Even our allies, like England and France, speak of their own problems and lack of internal support to give us any assistance. Only Canada and a few insignificant countries want to join with us in recovering from the disaster. It is only expected since they depend on us for defense and economy.

The greatest internal problem is looting. The day after the disappearance, numerous employees began taking the belongings of their fellow workers and bosses who vanished. By the next day, looters pillaged any place that was owned by someone who disappeared. They broke into homes, stores, and cars. My parents called me about my aunt and uncle in Colorado. They said a neighbor had called and told them my aunt and uncle's house was severely vandalized. They are going to drive out next month and check it out.

The economy has been stable considering all that has happened. Unemployment dropped to almost two percent as employers scrambled to fill the positions left by the disappearance. The only setback came from the New York Stock Exchange when it dropped over five hundred points due to all the confusion from the day before. It did, however, gain back over two hundred points within two days. Between the employment situation and the president's actions, the stock market is expected to increase even more than before. I have only a few shares from the exchange and they have already recovered from the drop.

I have yet to hear a solid explanation for the disappearance. A small segment believe that UFOs are behind everything. The greatest majority of them are atheists. It seems, though, that if it had been aliens, we would have heard something more from them by now. Why would they just come down and zap millions of people and then disappear without further communication? Not only that, but why would they only hit the U.S. and a couple other countries so hard, and the rest of the world so little, if at all?

The only other logical explanation would be that God took them out. This leaves only two alternatives. Either God removed the "fanatics" or God removed the evil. Both have explanations and possible proof. The New Agers (as they are now called) bring both into the most logical conclusion.

According to the New Agers, God removed all hindrances from our planet so we could reach a Utopia. This included the "evil" spirits, plus any people who would oppose the new age. They actually possess dated material of their predictions of the disappearance! At the present time, we are the beginnings of this Utopia, and will soon fully enter into this new age. Furthermore, they predict that God will send us Christ to teach us perfectly!

I don't know what to make of the New Agers' beliefs. I can handle a part of their explanations, but not all. I believe God took out the people and they will come back in the future. Their explanation of reaching a Utopia and sending us Christ seems a bit farfetched to me. I think that God simply wants us to believe in Him, and get our act together.

No matter what I think, the New Agers have grown greatly in numbers and power. Religions all over the world have focused in on their teachings. They possessed a great number of followers and believers in almost every country before the disappearance. Now, they seem to be dominating the beliefs of most people as the authority in the explanation of what has happened. What baffles most of us in the U.S. is how almost all the religions of the world have anticipated a Christ and the advancement of humans into a Utopia. These other religions point to Christianity as the stumbling block, and claim that is the reason the U.S. and other Christian countries were hardest hit from the disappearance!

Year One

Israel defeated Russia and all her allies today! The Soviets have officially withdrawn from the Middle East and renounced any more intentions of takeover. They leave like whipped puppies. Their departure marks the end of almost six months of war on earth. The entire event began eleven months ago, about two weeks after the disappearance.

After the initial shock of millions of people disappearing, the world continued with little concern (except for the United States, as I mentioned the last time I wrote). The three major events were the forming of the Federation, the beginning of the World Church, and the intensified energy crisis. Here in the United States, our economy and recovery required all our resources and attention. Thus, we withdrew financial aid and military forces from most foreign countries.

In the meantime, the European Common Market grew substantially, partially from the fall of the United States, and partially from their own consolidation. They officially formed a unified economic and military body, calling themselves "The Federation." This enhanced great respect from the only other military power, Russia. To ensure success, they quickly adopted the already present single money system as the official and only monetary exchange accepted. In addition, all the countries felt they needed an official president to run and moderate the Federation. They named one of the famous Habsbergs, an Austrian banker and financial tycoon, as their new leader. He was the unanimous choice of the Federation. probably due to his gentle approach to world peace, and because he was the single biggest factor in the entire setup of the monetary system and the smooth transition involved. His family's political influence did not hurt his bid for nomination either. They have all been very powerful and wealthy for many years.

Immediately after the summit meeting and the forming of the Federation, their new leader (nicknamed the Prince) began moving for peace and unification. His first stop was Israel for a peace treaty between the Federation and the Jews. They signed a seven-year agreement of peace and trade between the nations. The Federation needed the abundance of raw materials including oil, food, and minerals found in Israel for their climb to become the economic power of the world. On the other hand, Israel needed a strong economic power to trade their goods with, and maybe even more importantly, they could claim peace and sanction from the surrounding countries for the first time in their modern history. No one would dare to attack Israel with the Federation as an ally ... or would they?

The Prince's next stop was at the Vatican. He talked with the pope about many issues and both agreed that world peace should be the ultimate goal of religion and the Federation. He convinced the pope to hold a meeting of all the top religious leaders and try to unify into a one-world religion. The pope complied and invited all religious leaders to a world conference to be held at the Vatican. Some felt this was a move by the Prince to establish the religious center of the world (the Vatican) in the confines of the Federation's territory. However, others felt the move proved his desire to unify the world in peace by religion.

While the Prince pushed religious unification and peace, the energy crisis grew. Iran, Iraq, and even Saudi Arabia closed many dry wells. The United States' production fell dramatically as well. Oil companies and individuals searched for new oil findings everywhere. None were to be found. Gas prices skyrocketed to fifteen and twenty dollars a gallon here in the States. Elsewhere, the prices climbed to thirty and forty dollars a gallon, while in countries like Russia, Japan, and China, the only gas available went for government use.

Israel became the major supplier of oil in the world with production in the Arab nations dropping dramatically. Though oil had been discovered in Israel back in the Eighties, production was limited until the recent energy crisis. With the increased supply, Israel began exporting oil to the highest bidders. The Federation and the United States outbid other countries to receive their allocations. The poorer, underdeveloped countries like Russia and China received only small portions of oil from the smaller supplies in Iran and Iraq. The treaties signed by Israel with the Federation and the United States also garnered other small quantities of oil for domestic use.

Back at the Vatican, the conference of all the religious leaders provided the first ever unification of world religions. The meetings lasted several weeks, with mediation by the Prince. The two denominational giants, the established Catholic Church and the New Agers, need to agree and join together if there is any chance of having a world church. The New Agers have surpassed any other religion in numbers because of their explanation for the disappearance and their acceptance of all religions. According to reports, most Muslims and Hindus already follow the teachings of the New Age, for many of the New Age doctrines came from their Eastern philosophies. Unlike the old teachings of Muslims and Hindus, however, the New Age incorporates all other religions into their eternal plan as well. On the other hand, the Catholic Church claimed a billion devoted followers from around the world and was deep into their traditional values. If they did not conform in some ways, a world church would seem very unlikely.

The Prince played a large role in the discussions. According to the reports, he coordinated the adoption of bylaws for the one-world church. He proved influential in coercing the pope and the Catholic Church to adopt many of the New Ager's answers and ideas for the one-world church. In return, the New Agers allowed the pope to become the official spokesman of the new church. They felt that the new church needed a leader, and the pope could best fit into the leadership position. Thus, the two major religions united and the rest quickly agreed to the new proposals as they each were given some authority in the new church. They adopted the written bylaws as the World Church became the official world religion.

The following week, the pope televised the first service of the World Church. Billions from around the world gathered by television sets to hear the first sermon and the explanations of the disappearance. Through the computer interpreters each country heard his speech in its own language. Some of his comments caught my attention!

"... The World Church believes that God gathered home millions of people for the purpose of teaching them His ways. God also wanted a beginning for mankind to become the gods of this new age. In John chapter ten, verse thirty-four, Jesus Himself said we are gods .... All will be free to worship God in whatever way they choose. We will come to church and worship together as a unified body of believers. ... We will now refer to the disappearance as the new beginning. Join us in worship and together we will usher in the new age. The world can become a better place only if we join in spirit and mind. ... The World Church will begin appointing the largest church buildings throughout the world as the spiritual centers. Others will be built to accommodate heavily populated areas. At the end of my broadcast, a number will be given for you to call to find the spiritual center nearest you. There will be trained leaders to lead you in your own personal spiritual walk ..."

I watched the completion of the broadcast and my wife wrote down the number to call. She immediately began talking of the great things to come and how all the world problems would be solved. "Isn't this great!" she exclaimed. "We can now all worship together. No matter what race or background or denomination we had before, we can join together in prayer and step into this new age."

"I just don't know if it will be that easy," I remarked.

"Oh, come on, what more could you ask than having all these religions join together; and did you hear the explanation of the disappearance ... er, new beginning? It was incredible how precise they were about the details, even producing documented proof of their predictions, foretelling what has just happened!"

"I know those predictions are impressive, but I still don't think having a world religion will solve all the problems. And don't forget that not everyone has chosen this new religion yet. Over a billion people continue to be atheists or nonconformists. And don't forget all the people claiming to be Christ, too," I pointed out.

"True, but with almost five billion people following this new World Church already, it's only a matter of time!" she persisted.

"I hope you're right, but I just don't think it will be that easy."

My fears became reality about four months later, approximately six months after the disappearance. The Far East broke into fighting first. Revolutions and riots erupted in Korea, Indonesia, Japan, and China. Africa and South America followed with wars between several countries, causing great casualties. Mexico fell to the largest civil war in the world. The government begged the United States to send troops in to help. We quickly released thousands of soldiers into Mexico and South America to help the governments that needed it. The thousands turned into hundreds of thousands, and the Americans suffered millions of casualties in addition to the millions throughout the world.

Then the rumors began about Russia, the Federation, and Israel. Russian forces were reported to be moving into Lebanon along with forces from Libya, Iran, Iraq, Jordan, Egypt, Turkey, Ethiopia, and even Germany! Israel scrambled to protect itself from the imminent invasion. The United States, England, Canada, and a few other countries spoke against the Russian movements toward a takeover, but with no power to oppose any advancements, we were not taken seriously.

Everyone looked to the Prince for what the Federation would do. At first, he denied that Russia would even attack Israel. Within a month, the undeniable evidence of gathering armies in Lebanon caused him to state that the Federation would do nothing unless asked by Israel, and at that time the Federation would make a decision. Israel never did ask anyone for help. They struggled to put together forces that could stop the onslaught of armies coming.

Russian-led forces moved out of Lebanon and into northern Israel. Egyptian-led forces rolled through the Gaza Strip and northward into Israel. Millions of troops in trucks, tanks, on horses, and on foot journeyed beyond any fighting force since 1948. The lack of fuel for adequate use of tanks and vehicles proved insignificant as the armies swarmed upon the hills. Would Russia and her allies control the largest energy and mineral supply in the world? If the Federation did not aid Israel, who would?

The advancing troops were divided into three divisions of attack. The first division consisted of tanks and rocket launchers for blasting the defenses. The second division consisted of the large cavalry armed with rifles and spears for city capture and control. The third division contained only foot soldiers with bows and arrows and other hand weapons for silent executions of individuals throughout each city captured. They spread the troops throughout the countryside for efficient defense against any jets and missiles. When the Israeli jets flew over the front lines, they met many anti-aircraft guns and millions of troops spread all over the hills. Each missile killed only a few soldiers at a time, with many jets being knocked out. The invading forces were virtually unstoppable, even without a sufficient supply of modern weapons or gasoline for the vehicles.

Then, just when the entire invading army crossed into Israeli territory, an odd event changed history. A great earthquake rocked the foundations of the nation of Israel. The hills crumpled into oblivion, walls broke down into dust, tidal waves crashed upon the shores. Tremors were felt in every country on earth. The invading troops immediately fell to the ground, and began to fight with each other. Iranians fought Egyptians, Libyans battled Jordanians, and even the Russians feuded with one another. Then people became sick from an unknown pestilence. Thousands vomited and keeled over dead. Rain poured down upon the fields, creating mud and hindering any type of movement. Lightning filled the air and softball-sized hail dropped like miniature bombs. To top it off, burning sulfur, like acid rain, scorched the skin of all the allied forces. The Jews watched the entire ordeal from afar, not even touched by any of the natural phenomenon.

In horror, the armies tried to hide, but there was no

place to go. Out of all the vehicles, only the tanks could maneuver in the mud. They turned around and headed back to the border, but ran out of gas before reaching it. The cavalry and footmen fell victim to the elements and pestilence. Vainly they tried to run, but the mud denied access to freedom. In all, over thirty million troops died, with approximately six million surviving.

The Russians and her allies withdrew completely from Israel, and even Lebanon. They officially declared peace and recalled all military threats. The Jews rejoiced and sacrificed to their God for saving them. Now, for the first time since the Dark Ages, peace reigns upon earth!

In an unusual statement from the pope today, he warned Russia to join the World Church. "... It was a known fact that Russia continued to deny the presence of God. They have disregarded the World Church and the Federation's quest for peace. Maybe now, Russia, you will join with us, instead of against us ..."

The only other news is the sharp rise of inflation and unemployment in our country. At first, the disappearance left millions of jobs open. Companies paid outrageous salaries trying to entice people from other jobs to fill their vacancies. Other employees demanded pay raises for the extra work load caused by the disappearance. The unemployment rate dropped to almost zero for the first time in history. In turn, the companies raised prices to offset the wage increases. Making matters worse, gasoline prices continued to climb due to the energy crisis. Consequently, inflation rose dramatically and in one month alone, it climbed twenty-three percent!

The inflation rate far exceeded the wage hikes of just a few months back. People chose to horde the money they made instead of spending it, compounding the problem. In addition, several million buyers, having been taken off the planet, are now gone from the consumer market. Therefore, several large companies closed or laid off shifts, with others following suit. The unemployment rate now exceeds twenty-seven percent! Consider the inflation rate of sixty-one percent and one can imagine the economic situation for us.

I have been very fortunate so far. After the disappearance, several private companies offered me substantial wage increases to work for them. I discussed the offers of these other companies with the head of our division. He told me to wait a couple of days for him to see what he could do. Meanwhile, several of my key managers quit to work for private companies because the government could not promise an immediate raise. The problem with government jobs is all the red tape one must cut through to get anything accomplished. Luckily, most of the regular workers did not leave because the benefits and wages they received from the government still compared favorably with the offers of other companies.

Three days after meeting with my boss, he informed me of my fifteen thousand dollar pay increase per year. He also finagled pay increases for two other key personnel under us. My wife encouraged me to take one of the other offers, which amounted to almost forty thousand dollars more than the government could pay me.

"Honey," she began, "think of all the things we could do with that extra money. We could buy that house we looked at a few months ago, get some new furniture, and who knows how far up you could move from that position! You really cannot advance any farther in your government job."

"I know," I answered. "But I really like my job, and I have several years put in there. The extra money would be nice, but I have an uneasy feeling about leaving. Something isn't right."

"Well, I don't want you to leave for a job that you would dislike or that would demand more time away from home. I like having you around, especially with our new arrival coming soon. You are still young for your position. Who knows, you might end up in Washington someday!"

"No, thanks!" I retorted.

I was happy to have my wife back up what I thought all along. With our son entering school and another child on the way, I had enough family responsibility without the pressures of a new job. My wisdom paid off when, several months later, two of the three companies that had offered me jobs closed down. The other one went through major executive struggles. Even with another depression in the forecast, my job is secure and enjoyable.

One Year, Six Months

Thirty dollars for a loaf of bread! That is the price I had to pay today at our supermarket for just one loaf of bread. A can of corn costs over fifteen dollars! A good steak ranges between thirty and one hundred dollars! To buy a hamburger at any of the local fast-food places costs at least twenty. If buyers opt for the works (tomato, lettuce, pickles, and cheese), they will pay a premium twenty-seven dollars! Our only hope for a decrease will be this summer, after harvest.

Prices began rising around a year ago, during the wars. The combination of so many people going to war, the storms, and the drought, quickly lifted prices for food. Actually, we in the United States are very fortunate to have all the food we do. It may cost us a tremendous amount, but countries like Japan, South Africa, Mexico, and Spain have widespread famine. The expense for food surpasses the income of over half their residents. A program I watched last night reported on Japan's middle income class and how they are living on one meal of vegetables a day!

My wife and I have changed our eating habits like everybody else. We now eat only two meals a day. For breakfast, we enjoy two eggs (usually scrambled), two pieces of toast with butter, and a few glasses of grape juice. We do not drink coffee, because grape juice can be bought so reasonably. Dinner allows for a little larger meal. Beginning with chicken or some beef product, we then add a potato or some corn. To top it off, we indulge in grapes or an apple, and wash it all down with a glass of milk or wine. Since wine is so inexpensive compared with everything else, I drink it like I used to drink soda pop. Beer is out of the question, as a six-pack costs between seventy and ninety dollars! On rare occasions, my wife and I treat ourselves to ice cream or pie for dessert.

I must admit, I feel in better shape than I used to, due in large part to not eating anything between meals. With the price of snacks, no one can afford to eat them. A bag of microwave popcorn runs sixteen dollars! Once a week, I splurge and buy a bag of potato chips, a chocolate bar, and a soda pop, usually eating it Sunday afternoon, curled up in my favorite easy chair, while watching a football game. All in all, it's not that bad once you get used to it.

My wife looks better now than when we first married. She decided to begin her diet when the prices skyrocketed. In two months she lost over fifteen pounds and is in better shape than ever before. She pesters me about giving up snacks altogether. However, I will not give up my one snack a week, no matter how much she badgers me about it.

Eating out has become a treat rather than a necessity. A meal at a fast-food joint consisting of a burger, fries, and a soda pop, sells for forty dollars! To eat at a diner or restaurant with a waitress costs about fifty-five plus a tip! Actually, only a few restaurants remain in business. Quite common are signs in the windows stating, "Sorry, due to the extreme price of food, we are closed. Please come back when the famine is over." To think, only a few short months ago, I actually thought I needed to eat out because I deserved a break. Ha! Little did I realize what a privilege it was to eat out. All it took was a famine to reshape my thinking.

Our monthly food budget has gone out the roof. Two meals a day, plus one snack a week equals almost two thousand a month, not including the expense of eating out occasionally. I've thought about eliminating our privilege of eating out once a month, but hey, my wife and I deserve some luxuries every so often. If we get real desperate, we can always cut out breakfast.

I must admit, I'm luckier than most. Thanks to my job, I can still afford the extravagant meals. So many others in our country can afford only one meal a day. My neighbors down the street live on one meal of vegetables and fruit a day. The man lost his job at a factory after they laid off two shifts. His wife found a job at a retail store in a mall for their only source of income. They may lose their house soon if he doesn't find some work. Others with big families are literally beginning to starve.

Down in the city, it's common to see children as young as four or five years old begging for food. I tried to give one a dollar today, but she asked for food instead. She could not have been older than seven or eight. Her sky-blue eyes and washed, golden blonde hair contrasted with her whimperish voice. She said, "A dollar won't buy me anything for my family. Do you have any food that we could eat?"

I replied, "Do I look like a walking grocery store? Here, take five dollars."

She slowly lifted her hand, wondering at my sincerity. I smiled as she took it and mumbled, "Thanks."

I watched for a moment as she walked to another businessman. I could not hear the girl's request, but the man turned the other way and walked off without a smile. She moved on down the street and I continued toward the grocery store to pick up a few items for my wife.

I did not understand how people could just turn away from a young girl begging for food. My heart went out to her. I know my five dollars would not help a lot, but it might be just enough for her to make it one more day. And maybe that one day could be the break in this famine. If we would all chip in equally, I bet almost everyone would survive until the famine diminished. Yet, so few are willing to give for the survival of human lives just because they do not want to lower their standard of living.

As I contemplated the lack of compassion, I noticed a throng of people gathered around the supermarket. Approximately fifty people stood at the front doors arguing with a man dressed in a white apron. The man shouted, "If you do not leave my premises, I'll call the police!"

"We have no other way to get food!" one exclaimed.

"I'm sorry, but I've lost enough customers already. They have complained about being harassed when leaving my store. I have to make a living or I'll be begging for my family. Please leave immediately or I'll call the police."

Slipping through the crowd, I walked past the man. The automatic doors swung open, and I sighed with relief. I didn't want to get mixed up in that ordeal whatsoever. Turning the corner, I walked toward the disposable diaper aisle.

Most of the shelves in the store were empty. The produce department had only a small selection of vegetables and fruit. Dust covered the display cases and the machines in the bakery department. Stopping at the meat counter, I gazed at the minuscule selection. Forcing myself to move on, I picked up the diapers and a loaf of bread, knowing we could not splurge on a steak until next week. From in front, the automatic doors opened and loud voices began to penetrate the peacefulness. "I'm calling the police!"

"Go ahead, we're going to die anyway!"

I walked past the end of the aisle and into two men. "Excuse me," remarked one as they grabbed several packages from the shelves.

The crowd moved from outside the store, entering through the doors. Moving briskly, they snatched whatever they could carry in their arms. The man with the apron jumped behind the counter and ducked down. Standing up with a rifle in his hand, he grabbed the phone and his voice echoed throughout the building. "If you try to leave without paying for the food, you will be shot!"

Frozen from fear, I stood next to the checkout counter, not sure whether to move toward the cashier or just wait to see what happened. A wailing siren approached from outside and I decided it would be wise to wait. The crowd hurriedly filtered back toward the doors, unable to run because of the loads in their arms.

The man yelled at the top of his voice to the first group approaching the door, "Please don't make me shoot!"

I winced as the man took aim and shot the first person coming to the door. From the force of the bullet, the man fell sideways into the wall as the food he carried flew in different directions. No one stopped. Another shot dropped a woman to the floor. The desperate crowd quickened its pace, each hoping they would be the lucky ones to escape with their bounty. Two more shots found their mark with the bodies falling in front of the throng fast approaching the door. The first police car screeched to a stop outside the store. Several other sirens approached the fracas, while the man continued to fire into the crowd.

I heard the policeman from outside order, "Halt! Police! We will shoot if you do not stop!"

At least two other guns began firing from outside. The man from behind the counter shot the last person trying to make it out the door. He hopped over the counter with his gun firmly grasped in his hand. The police continued shooting for a moment and then stopped. The man stepped over one of the bodies and walked out the door.

A deafening silence fell upon the store. I could not believe what I had just witnessed. A moan from one of the bodies in front broke the stillness. A gray-haired woman, with features hardened by many years of labor, came out from behind the counter. She walked up to the mess and began picking up the food spread across the floor, completely ignoring several slowly moving bodies and their grunts for help.

The man with the gun came back in with two policemen following. He walked to the counter, leaned over, and picked up a box of ammunition. He reloaded his gun with several bullets, while the policemen stood by the door talking quietly with each other. The man aimed at one of the moving bodies on the ground.

"Wait!" I yelled. Instinctively, I jumped to the aid of the wounded bodies.

The gun fired. I stopped in my tracks. The gun fired again. "No!" I gasped in horror.

He fired two more times and the moaning stopped. While I stared in shock, more shots were fired from outside. Looking out of the window, I saw one of the policemen kick a body, step back, and fire his gun into it, like a hunter over his prey.

My vision blurred with a tunneling effect. Drawing in several deep breaths, I leaned against a checkout counter. Slowly, I regained my vision and put down my belongings on the conveyer belt. The lady stopped collecting the food to come to my assistance. She rang up the purchases as if unaffected by the horror of moments ago.

After paying, I picked up my bag and headed to my car. I could not help looking down at the victims sprawled across the floor. Gagging several times, I quickly tried to step through the door, only to slip in a pool of blood, almost falling onto one of the bodies. I closed my eyes and ran outside to escape the tragedy. Once outside, an unusual smell caught my nostrils. Gazing down, two bodies in a pool of blood lay before me. I staggered over the bodies and past the policemen, heaving several times. Reaching a nearby car, I stopped to catch my breath.

One of the policeman came over and asked, "Are you all right?"

"I will be in a minute," I gasped. "I just needed to get outside and breathe some fresh air."

After a few moments, I questioned the officer, "Why did you kill the ones still alive?"

"Because we don't have room in any of the hospitals or prisons. They also don't have any extra food to feed them. To lock up people like this, or even treat them at a hospital, would cost more money than the state can afford."

"Come on!" I shouted. "We're talking about human life here!"

"Listen, pal!" he commanded. "If we did not do this, you would not have the stuff you're holding now. Mobs of people have begun storming the stores. We have no way of stopping them, or anywhere to put them. They grab what they can and run. If we catch four or five, we've done great. The only problem is, that means forty people get away. When we do this, we retrieve most of the food, plus scare the rest of the people from trying to do it again. If you can come up with a better way, call the chief!"

He turned away and walked back to his fellow officers. I saw him shake his head and point back toward me. The others looked and shook their heads. They laughed and continued their conversation.

I didn't know what to think. The horrors of just moments ago, all of a sudden seemed right. But, how could just outright murdering people be okay? Yet, if they hadn't shot the rioters, they would have come back in a day or two and done the same thing again. That would mean the grocery store would close and I would not be able to buy any food. That wouldn't be right either, would it?

I told my wife about it at home. She could not believe that they murdered the crowd, either. She even became frantic and worried about going to the store to shop for anything. I reassured her I would do anything she needed to get done if she felt unsafe.

Writing now, I still feel remorse about the entire incident. I have replayed the whole thing in my mind a hundred times. If there was something I could have done, I sure don't know what it could have been. It seems almost inevitable that these incidents will take place while the famine continues. But, deep down my instincts warn me of danger or of something wrong. I sense that something is strange and out of place.

Besides the famine, the world watches the Federation and its leader, the Prince. At this point, no country or group of countries can match up with the Federation in any economic or military threat. Russia and her allies are still licking their wounds from the battle in Israel. China continues its *laissez-faire* attitude because of the famine and internal problems. The United States has no power to do anything because of the continuing recovery from the disappearance. Only Israel would seemingly be strong enough to oppose the Federation. They, however, seem content to sacrifice to their God and not bother with the rest of the world. One thing is clear; though they are small and seemingly insignificant, no one will dare to oppose them anymore after the Russian war.

The only other major news item involves the growing World Church. The Prince announced that the Federation had voted to adopt the World Church as the only religion. This did not come as a surprise to most. With the pope being the official statesman for the World Church, and the headquarters now in Rome, it made sense to have the greatest military power contain the biggest and most powerful religion in the world. Now, the Federation unquestionably is the greatest military power, biggest economic power, and the most influential religious power.

Oddly enough, three countries did vote against it. The presidents of England, Belgium, and the Netherlands opposed the new law. They did not state specific reasons for voting against the law, but some people feel that this is the continuation of their disagreement on the Prince's programs. They do not like his obvious influence on the World Church, and they feel he is doing this to benefit himself in religious affairs. The pope replied concerning the Prince's influence by saying, "... Anyone who wants unification and the betterment of the human race will always be heard by us."

I do not know what to think about the World Church, although my wife adamantly supports the unified church and hopes the United States will adopt it as the only religion. She desires to raise our children in an atmosphere exempt from religious conflicts, feeling this will eliminate the manipulation of our children by opposing views, which in turn might cause inner turmoil. With the riots, famines, and economic slumps so characteristic of today's society, she feels both of our children need the stability of uniting in just one religion with everyone else.

I looked upon the round little face of our newborn baby daughter. Her nose twitched and her eyes squinted when I blew playfully on her face. Her giggles and bright grin brought a smile to my lips. With the world trying to unite under one religion, and all the talk of a new world order, I know my growing family's future is a bright one!

Two Years

Death surrounds all of us like the fear of a child walking to school while the neighborhood bully follows close behind. There is no escaping the anxiety. You can pretend not to care. Even laugh it off. In the eyes of your friends, you are not afraid, but inside, the fear wrenches your stomach into knots because you know your time will come soon. You wake up with trepidation. You go to sleep wondering if you will awake. I can feel its omnipresence drawing close to me. Death is knocking at the door. Don't answer ... maybe it will go away.

The funeral for our neighbor is tomorrow. She died yesterday in the hospital, once again bringing home the reality of death. The doctors say it probably happened due to a combination of stress and malnutrition. Her husband was quite emotional about the whole ordeal. He came over after it happened and just talked about the last couple of weeks. Apparently, she had grown weaker each day from the demands of work and the lack of food. About a week ago, she caught a cold that never left. Although I assured him that he had no control over what happened, he kept blaming himself that she died. He asked me to ride with him in the procession and be a pallbearer.

Why me? I don't want to go to a funeral, much less be in the procession. I'm tired of seeing death. I'm tired of listening about it, and I'm definitely not interested in being around it. I wish I didn't have such a soft heart. Then I would have been able to tell him no instead of agreeing.

Actually, having a funeral at a funeral home is quite

unique these days. Due to the great demand from all the deaths, funeral homes raised the cost of their services, making it unaffordable for most middle-income families. Only the rich and special friends of the mortician can book a time with the funeral homes. My neighbor is having a normal funeral for his wife because his uncle is a mortician.

Most Americans now use the mini-funeral parlors that are springing up quicker than the fast-food chains did in the Seventies and Eighties. They pick up the body by station wagon, cremate it upon arrival at the parlor (to prevent spreading of disease), put it in a small remembrance room for one day, and allow people to give their last respects. Some parlors have drive-up windows for people to give their last respects in an even quicker service. They eliminate the need for huge funeral rooms, the embalming procedures, the expensive caskets, and other related costs. All this combined reduces the overall price to where the middle-income families can afford some sort of service for their deceased loved ones. They also significantly reduce the time needed for one to dwell upon death.

In other countries around the world, they gather corpses together and bury them in huge piles similar to the burial of Jews in World War II. In India and China, trucks travel down the streets while men in rubber suits gather the bodies and fling them into the back. Later, a mass of carcasses is dumped into huge holes and bulldozed over with dirt. As one can imagine, the diseases spread quickly due to the unsanitary conditions.

Around the globe, the death count rises. I believe it's now over one billion people that have died this last month. That's right ... over one billion! The unknown plague ravages every country, with no known cure. The famine and subsequent animal attacks claim countless lives. Most point to the famine as the reason for the vicious animal attacks. Not being able to find sufficient food, the animals resort to hunting humans in an effort to satisfy their appetites.

Yesterday, one of my assistants went with me to a business meeting in a town about forty miles from here. We arrived early and decided to pick up something for lunch. Trying to find a restaurant open for lunch was not an easy task. We finally found one on the outskirts of the other side of town. I parked the car by a telephone at the edge of the parking lot to make a quick call back to the office. My assistant opened his door and began walking around the car to meet me. From the corner of my eye, I caught a glimpse of a pack of dogs running full speed toward the car. I yelled, "Bob! Dogs!"

Taking a step toward the car, I grabbed the door handle. Locked. The growling dogs approached from the side. I fumbled for my keys and instinctively jumped on top of my car. My right leg jerked to the side as the first dog bit into my shoe while leaping to catch me. My hands grabbed the gutter on the other side of my roof and I pulled myself on top. A gun shot from the building caused a dog to yelp. Several others gathered in a pile on top of my assistant. Before I could react, a collie bounded to the hood of my car and growled fiercely as it sprung into the air toward me. I brought my arm down in front of my face, awaiting the impact. Another gun shot came from the building and the head of my attacker jolted sideways. The collie landed on my feet and slid down the window, leaving a trail of blood smeared all the way down to the ground as its body fell limp. As more shots came from the building, the dogs began to drop all around us.

Within moments it ended. My assistant screamed for only a moment after the guns ceased firing. Five people carrying rifles jogged to the car. Looking down, I saw several dogs lying in a pool of blood. Bob began sobbing, crawled to the door, and pulled himself onto his feet. The five men arrived, asking us if we were okay.

"I'm fine," I replied. "Bob, are you okay?"

"Yes," he quivered, "but they bit me hard on my legs and my arm."

"Come on inside; we'll fix you up!" bellowed a robust, bearded man dressed in overalls.

"You were lucky we saw them coming!" quipped another of the armed men in a jovial voice, "Or you would have been dinner instead of having some!"

"We are very grateful to you for saving us," I replied.

"No problem. They just would have attacked someone else later," answered the bearded man.

I slid off the car and began shaking the hands of our rescuers. They shook my hand, but gave more notice to my companion's wounds. Bob's clothes had been torn up severely, and blood flowed freely from several gashes on his arms and legs. The man led us into the diner and a waitress helped clean my assistant's clothes and wounds.

We invited the men to eat lunch with us. They gratefully accepted as we treated them to a hamburger and glass of water each. We discussed the animals' ferocious attacks on humans in their city and throughout the world. They told us how people around their town always carried guns, and never traveled alone for fear of being mauled. As we left, the men promised to contact us if they found any of the dogs to be rabid.

As I drove home that night, my mind somehow began to reflect on a sermon given by the pope last year. It was his first sermon as the official spokesman of the newly adopted World Church and religion of the Federation. At that time, I did not accept the explanation for the disappearance, though I did not deny it. I was not ready to believe anything so easily, and too much was happening too fast. I like to logically think out all possibilities before making any decision. Besides, just a few months after the pope's speech, wars broke out, initially dampening my thoughts on the reality of his words. But, as I drove down the lonely freeway, a small light began shining in my mind.

Many of the beliefs and ideas the pope presented did not make much sense, nor did they seem possible at the time. The complete uniting of all religions throughout the world was unrealistic, especially with so many atheists and agnostics. However, as of now, every country in the world has World Church Spiritual Centers in them. Any country that wants financial aid from the Federation must adopt the World Church as its official religion. The United States is close to adopting the World Church as our official religion for financial and trade purposes, yet some traditionalists still do not want our country to leave the foundations it was built on.

The other major belief the pope taught was the idea of the earth going through a trial period before we reached a Utopia. He explained how God had started the evolutionary ladder. Over the billions of years after the earth formed, we had progressed upward to the state of man. The time had come to take the next step up the ladder and evolve into gods. God removed certain hindrances from earth (the disappearance) so that we could progress. This progression to a Utopia would also involve a trial period commonly referred to as natural selection. Only the strongest and best suited for the progression would live through the trial.

I turned into the driveway and parked the car. Walking up the front steps, I could see a light in the living room. My wife had been pestering me for almost a year about going to the World Church. She would be happy about my decision to go to church, but how she would react to the dog attack of today I didn't know.

To my surprise, she handled the news of the dog

attack quite well. The shock and concern I expected her to have was overshadowed by her excitement about my decision to begin going to church on a regular basis. I explained my thoughts on how I could now see the famine and deaths as being a part of the natural selection process. She became almost ecstatic as I explained my thoughts. She had wondered about the problems the world was going through, and my thoughts helped her to realize why they existed. We took our son and daughter for a walk around the neighborhood that night, momentarily forgetting the problems surrounding us. The hope for the future calmed us as we envisioned how awesome the world would soon become.

That night, while I was lying in bed, my mind began recollecting the events of the day. The dog attack. The upcoming funeral. The wonderful evening I shared with my wife and two children. Then the horrifying thought hit me. What if my wife or kids did not make it through the trial? What if I didn't make it through? Trepidation swept over me once again. I didn't want to die! I didn't want my wife or children to die. How would I know if we would all make it through to the new world?

I looked over at my wife. She looked so peaceful as she slowly breathed in and out. Why did I feel doom all around us?

Two Years, Six Months

The Prince brings hope and anticipation to a world of despair. Plans and organizations thrive under his direction. His genius in military, economic, and religious affairs is unmatched. His oratorical abilities far surpass those of Winston Churchill, Jesus of Nazareth, or even the pope. He can bring into agreement an entire group of people opposed to each other. At points, he even uses the threat of power to influence a compromise between parties. I wonder whether or not he has more power than we give him credit for.

No other leader in the history of the world has had such an influence in the lives of all mankind. One thinks of Nebuchadnezzar and how he once had complete military control of the world. He, however, had little knowl edge of religion, and failed to control all parts of the world at the same time. Without mass communication and travel, his power was limited. In religious affairs, one must consider Jesus of Nazareth and how his teachings still influence millions of people two thousand years later. But he never controlled the world, nor did he have any political clout whatsoever. (If he had, he never would have died on the cross.) The Prince has not yet gained complete power in military or religious affairs, but he holds more influence in the overall sense than either Jesus or Nebuchadnezzar.

His political power cannot be denied anymore. Every nation in the world depends upon his world monetary system. With only one currency accepted by the Federation (developed by the Prince), each country must adhere to the regulations stipulated by them. In addition, just about every nation is indebted to the Federation. After the wars and famine, the world turned to the Federation for economic relief. At any point, the Federation could ruin a given country by cutting them out of the world monetary system and denying them access to the currency exchange headquarters located in the Federation.

One might wonder why the Federation would back him so adamantly. The answer is twofold. First, he has brought them into being the premier world power. They have superior economic strength, plus military power unmatched by any other country. Second, his banks originally developed the world currency. The computer headquarters are in one of his banks and he outright controls the Federation reserve, as well as the world cash supply.

This became apparent recently when three presidents opposed some of his plans. It began when the Federation adopted the World Church as the official religion. England, Belgium, and the Netherlands not only opposed the new law, but openly defied it. They also opposed the Prince in some of his dealings with other nations. The Prince called the three presidents to a special meeting with him. After the meeting, the three presidents spoke of his threats to extinguish their trade with the rest of the Federation and block it with other countries. They would not budge on what they thought was the right thing to do. The Prince then ordered the banks to shut off their transactions with the three countries.

With bankruptcy and depression facing the three nations, they immediately held special sessions and asked for another meeting with the Prince and their own selected representatives. The Prince agreed to meet with them as long as the three presidents would not be allowed to attend. After the meetings, the Prince told the news reporters that an agreement had been reached.

He would reinstate the three countries into the banking system, but the three presidents were to be replaced. Their successors were to be picked by the Prince and approved by the countries. They also agreed to enforce the World Church as the state religion. The representatives came out and expressed their approval of the agreement. All were happy that the Federation would not be interrupted by the incident and felt the removal of the previous presidents was in the best interest of all.

The Prince's degree of religious influence cannot be fully known or agreed upon. Some think that he has little say in the affairs of the World Church, for the pope and the delegates rule with no interference. Others think he controls it almost completely. Whatever the case, no one can deny that the Prince brought the World Church into its pinnacle of power through his support. Any country not promoting the World Church as the one world religion will face isolation by the Federation and all other countries. This, of course, pressures the countries into conforming for the sake of economic survival. I think most countries have willingly received the World Church anyway, without needing any threats.

Only a few countries, such as Russia, Israel, England, Belgium, and the Netherlands, opposed having the World Church established as the state religion. Otherwise, just about all others readily conformed—and why not? They have the only logical explanation for the new beginning. They unite everyone in one belief, which results in less tension amongst nations and ethnic groups. With or without these reasons, people are flocking to the World Church by the billions. Every major denomination joined with the World Church long ago. Thus, other religious sects have all melted away except two. The Jews continue to sacrifice to their God under Old Testament laws, and a small group profess Jesus Christ as the Messiah and that He is returning to set up His kingdom.

The entire situation with Israel is a strange one. The Prince will not force Israel to establish the World Church as their religion (though there are World Church Spiritual Centers set up in the country). Most believe it is due to them being the only country on earth not dependent upon the Federation for support. As a matter of fact, it seems that the Federation is more dependent upon Israel for oil and other exports than Israel is upon them. Some speculate this is the reason for the Prince's carefree attitude toward their religious practices. Others hold the belief that the Prince is actually a Jew, but when asked, the Prince will neither confirm nor deny it. The Prince himself explains his actions as being a result of the seven-year treaty signed by Israel and the Federation. Furthermore, he added that the Jewish practices do not violate the World Church's doctrine.

For whatever reason, the Federation and Israel have a unique relationship. With the devastation of Russia, plus their treaty with the Federation, Israel has no threat of an invasion. They seem to want no part in world affairs, just to be left alone in peace for the first time since the famed King Solomon's reign. The Prince refuses to interfere with their religion and state affairs, but insists upon Federation troops being dispatched around all exports of goods. Federation troops are also assigned to the World Church Spiritual Centers to ensure their freedom. One of the main spiritual centers is in the old Muslim mosque on top of the Dome of the Rock, which is within yards of the new temple that the Jews rebuilt for their sacrifices.

The Jews seem unconcerned by the presence of the Federation troops. They have no real need to be concerned. They outnumber them ten to one. If any threat of invasion were to occur, the Israelis could easily subdue the troops already in their nation. After what happened to the Russians and her allies, the Federation wouldn't dare to attack Israel.

The only other religious group left on earth is the Kingdom Preachers (as they are commonly referred to). However, they are diminishing quickly due to the executions begun by the World Church. This group believes that Jesus Christ is going to set up His kingdom on the earth and reign from it. They also speak of more harsh judgments rather than easier ones.

In opposition, the World Church announced a few months ago that anyone openly against the unification of the religious world would be put to death. Although not openly stated, this proclamation was aimed strictly at the Kingdom Preachers and anyone who professed Jesus Christ as the only Lord. The Prince gave his support and encouragement to all nations joining forces to rid themselves of these troublemakers. About two weeks ago, the executions began, and due to the adoption of the World Church as our official religion, the United States is also taking part.

The authorities gather the Kingdom Preachers together at the execution centers. Each one is given a chance to recant. If they choose not to deny Jesus Christ as the only God, they are slain. If they confess that we are developing into gods and soon will be one, they are freed. People are still allowed to worship Jesus if they so choose (one of the World Church's doctrines), but may not preach of His judgments nor that He is the only God to worship.

Until the executions began, I tried not to talk about religion with anyone. Unfortunately, after one of my employees became a so-called Christian just two or three months ago, he began preaching about Jesus coming back and setting up His kingdom. When the news of the executions came, other employees warned him of the possibility of dying. With that in mind, he continued more fervently to tell everyone over and over about our doom.

Many of my employees asked me to fire him because his boss would not. I talked to his boss and asked him what he thought of the situation. He told me that he couldn't fire the man because of the great work he started to do just after his supposed experience. Though he continually talked about the experience, his work actually surpassed that of everyone else. He had no reason to fire him except for the religious aspect.

When the news came in about the executions, I knew the time had come to talk with him before he jeopardized the entire division. I thought about what to say, but my heart wasn't with my mouth.

"You understand why I called you in here, don't you?" I asked.

"Yes, sir," he replied.

I noticed he sat in a confident manner. He leaned toward me as he spoke and his eyes beamed with boldness. A slight smile leaked from his lips.

"Maybe you don't quite understand the full implication," I started. "Not only is your job in jeopardy, but your life is at stake ... Jeff, your life is about to end if you are not wise!"

"I understand, sir, but I am ready to die for my Savior Jesus Christ," he boldly proclaimed.

"Listen, Jeff, I really admire your boldness in your beliefs, but don't be a fool. It won't do any good from the grave. Once you die, that's it. No more. Finished. What good will it do you then to believe in Jesus?"

"Well, sir, not to show any disrespect for you, but my life on earth has already ended and my new life will be made manifest when I die."

I leaned back and thought for a moment, trying to understand where he was coming from. He seemed to actually look forward to dying. He also thought that Jesus gave him a new life. I wanted to know why he thought this.

"Okay," I breathed, "let's cut the formality. I know you used to be a real party person. You drank and I heard rumors about your affairs and how you were taking drugs. You came into work with hangovers every Monday and used to tell dirty jokes and make passes at just about every woman in the office. Tell me about your religious experience. I want to know."

"Sir, I have looked forward to this moment for a long time. I have desired to tell you my story since everything happened. I have been praying that I would have the opportunity to tell you my story." He sat back in the chair and began. "I never went to church when I grew up. My parents were atheists. I had nothing in this life to live for but to party, and to try to work my way up to a prestigious position like you have. I wanted to live life to the fullest. But, when the disappearance happened, I started to wonder about its religious aspect. At first, I ran from it and partied even more."

"Then one day, this guy came to me and asked if I had ever heard of Jesus Christ. I said I had, but I really didn't know who He was. He then told me that Jesus Christ died on the cross for me and all my sins. Not only that, but He rose from the grave to prove He was God. He explained to me that Jesus was the one who took everyone off the earth at the disappearance. He then brought out the Bible and showed me the events that we are going through right now in the book of Revelation. I was amazed. The Bible tells exactly what has happened so far, and what will come next! He then read more scripture telling of Jesus' coming kingdom and the doom for all those that won't trust in Him as their personal Savior."

Jeff continued, "He then asked me if I wanted to take part in this new kingdom, or if I would rather end up in the lake of fire for eternity. I quickly told him that I wanted to be in the kingdom. He then warned me that when I trusted in Jesus Christ as my personal Savior, I would end up having to die for Him and could never receive the mark from the Prince (if I would live that long, which he said would be doubtful according to the Bible). I thought for a moment, and decided that I wanted to be forgiven for all my sins. Besides, if I didn't accept Christ, I knew I would have just over four years before I would die when Jesus returned . . . if I made it that long.

"At that time, I accepted Jesus Christ as my personal Savior and asked Him to cleanse me from all the sins I've ever done and ever would do before His return. I knew then that I would live eternally, though I would die in this physical body. Jesus loved me enough to die on the cross so that I could live eternally. To die for Him is really to live for Him. I know that I must tell everyone I can about this free gift. What about you? May I show you verses on what I've been talking about?"

"No, not now. Thanks anyway, though," I replied.

What could I say? I've heard about that all before in church. I remember my pastor and I talking about it one evening at a dinner. He asked me about being a Christian. I told him that I believed in Jesus and that I had been baptized when I was younger. He never asked me about it again. Of course, the pastor had disappeared along with many other church members. Then why weren't some of the others, or even myself, taken away by Jesus if He was the one who did it? Why wouldn't I be included?

I wondered about how this man sitting in front of me could really know that he would be with Jesus when he died. He talked about how personal everything was to him. I didn't remember anything so personal happening to me like he described. Maybe that's what's missing. On the other hand, what if Jesus really isn't God? Then

I would waste my life like he was, off into oblivion forever. What good would that be?

I've lived a good life. If there really is a heaven with Jesus up there, He knows how hard I've tried to be a Christian. I'm sure that He wouldn't make me burn in a lake of fire. After all, I never did half the things this guy did.

"Please, let me show you the verses about how much Jesus loves you and how you can have the free gift," Jeff said, interrupting my thoughts.

"No thanks, I've already read about it and heard it in church. This isn't the time or place. Besides, you're about to die for those beliefs. You're the one who should be listening," I said, coming back to reality.

I realized the doubts I was having were because of messages preached before in church. I felt the same now as back then. I believed them to an extent, just not quite like he did. I just wasn't ready to make such a final decision. I've always been one to think about all the possibilities. Of course, I've had many years to make the decision since the first time I faced it in church. I'm just not ready to die like Jeff was.

A knock on the door from one of my managers ended our discussion. He wanted to leave the Bible for me to read, but I told him I had one at home. As he left, he encouraged me to read it.

I did not see him again before his execution. He left me his personal Bible with a note attached saying how he hoped I would trust in Jesus as my personal Savior.

I don't understand the need to execute those who believe differently than the World Church. He did no harm to anyone with his beliefs. I believed close to the same way, just not to the extent he did. I'm just not stupid enough to throw away my life here on earth for something that might be false. Besides, the world is really coming around into a better place to live thanks to the hard work and foresight of the Prince. Of all the people in the world to emulate and listen to, he's head and shoulders above the rest.

Along with the great leadership and oratorical abilities, his personal life shines as one with a deep desire to bring unity and peace for the betterment of all people. Unlike so many other politicians and leaders, his life has never been marred with an affair. He isn't married and seems to be disinterested in having any relationship. When asked by a reporter if he had a secret girlfriend, he replied by saying he did not have time to get involved in a romance with so many pressing problems facing the earth.

He continues to urge all to go to the World Church and worship. No matter what town he visits, on Sunday morning he brings his entire group to the World Church to worship. He will honor any god of any country so long as they want to bring unity and peace to our planet. He gives many presents to each worship center he visits. Gold and silver statuettes with diamonds and incense are his favorite gifts to give.

His work the last two years in the final restoration of Babylon as the center of trade for all countries proves his desire of unifying the world by economic means. Each country maintains and uses a section of the city for purposes of selling their products to buyers. The Federation armies guard and protect all ships and planes coming in and out. No trade restrictions or taxes are imposed, just the lease payments for each country's section in the city. Now, every country has equal opportunity to buy and sell goods in a common, free territory.

I know the world still faces many problems, but with the Prince leading the way, our unification should end most of them. The pope preaches about making it through the fire into our Utopia. After the wars, drought, and great plague of deaths, our world can only improve!

Even I am beginning to think so.

Three Years

A very frightening event happened to me around six p.m. today. I was sitting outside on our porch after work, sipping on lemonade and enjoying the cool of the evening. I began feeling uneasy ... sort of odd; the feeling one receives when something bad is about to happen. Looking around, I could see nothing out of the ordinary. Leaning back, I took another sip of the refreshing drink and could tell that it was darker. Setting my drink down, I rubbed my eyes. There was no mistaking it now, the sky was darker. The sun looked orange, like when it was setting. Except, sunset was still two hours away.

I stepped down off the porch while continuing to rub my eyes and looking around. The automatic street lights had clicked on above me. Other people were walking out of their homes and looking at the sky. Then I saw a star ... and another! They began popping out like a fast-motion sunset. The moon came out and turned to a deep, dark red! I slowly turned toward the sun, catching the last glimmer of light, before the eclipse blackened the sky!

Suddenly, the ground shook as if a train were approaching. I began to shake with the earth below me and fell to my hands and knees. Everything shook back and forth, and buildings around me blurred into one massive shaking object. Piercing screams could barely be heard over the low rumbling noise, and I thought of only one thing... hide! I staggered to my feet and started taking steps. Bright flashes of light exploded around me. I could see the white streaks coming straight down as if they were shooting at me. The stars caused a strobe light effect as I ran down the street, covering my head with my arms. This had to be a nightmare, I hoped.

Tripping on something, I sprawled across the street face first. Blood slowly formed in droplets on my scraped hands. One is not supposed to feel pain in a dream, I thought. Amidst the flashes of light, other people ran around covering their heads. The screams were drowned out by the increasing rumbling noises below me. Everyone was running to hide … but where?

In the confusion and commotion, my mind panicked. I thought God was coming to destroy us. No one could stand against His power. I figured He was angry because no one acknowledged Him for anything we had. I felt exposed. He could see me. I dropped my head between my knees and wouldn't look up to the sky. I wanted to hide in a cave from the fear of facing God.

Crouching back on my knees, I positioned myself to jump up and try to run. Then, it stopped. The screaming lasted only a couple of seconds longer. Silence. A relieved silence. The sky began to brighten. First it turned a purplish red, brightening quickly to orange, then a deep blue, and finally to normal sky blue. The stars vanished as quickly as they had appeared. I heard cars start up and horns blowing.

Standing up, I realized I was about two blocks away from my house. Turning around, I started back home, walking in a lackadaisical state, feeling as if I had just awakened from a bad dream. Other people sat on the ground with their heads in their hands, or looking up into the sky. Others walked around their homes, inspecting for damage. My pace quickened as I thought about the damage to my house and whether my wife was unharmed.

My wife sat crying outside on the front porch. As our eyes met, she sprang up and ran to me. We embraced for a short time and started walking around the house with our arms around each other. I finally broke the silence when I noticed a crack in the foundation of our house. As we talked about it for a minute and continued the stroll, we noticed another large crack in our driveway. We went inside to study the break in our house's foundation, and decided to have it professionally repaired. She said she would call first thing in the morning.

I have not yet told her how I felt when the earthquake hit. We just discussed how much damage it might have done. Maybe we are both apprehensive to express our feelings. The less I think about what happened, the better I feel.

The late night news reported on the worldwide earthquake and the devastation left behind. Not even one country escaped the violent shaking. New York, London, Moscow, Delhi, and Tokyo all suffered great damage and casualties. Several skyscrapers received irreparable damage to their foundations. In Italy, the famed Leaning Tower of Pisa finally fell to its destruction. No one even ventured a guess as to the total dollar amount of damage; they would only say it was billions and billions of dollars worth.

In our city, thousands of homes were destroyed and countless others suffered damage of some sort. One large building downtown collapsed into the street, killing over one hundred people. The State Bank's entire second floor collapsed into the lobby. Luckily, only a few were left in the bank and no one was killed. Our neighborhood escaped with little damage. The foundation of one house broke in half and another had a wall cave in, but no one was hurt. Everyone else, like myself, suffered minor damage in their homes that can be repaired.

Of the entire event of the day, one question remained unanswered. Where was the epicenter? The experts cannot pinpoint a place where the earthquake came from. Every measurement of the earthquake around the world reported a seven on the Richter scale. Many seismologists believe the epicenter actually was the middle of the earth. Others venture to say that there was actually no epicenter at all. Whatever the case, I still think God took part in the event of today.

It was the first major incident since the death plague of last year. Until today, the world was running along quite smoothly and recovering from the earlier catastrophes. Famine still persists throughout the land, but most have learned to cope with one to two meals a day. The jobless rate in the United States dropped to recession instead of depression figures. The World Church thrives with no opposition (all the Kingdom Preachers that we know of have been eliminated) and the Prince continues his unification policy. The only trouble stems from the Russians and Egyptians.

Reports from both countries speak of their disdain toward Israel and the Prince. Some speculate the dislike of the Prince's role in the World Church as the main reason for the animosity. Others venture to guess the treaty between Israel and the Federation brings too much control over world affairs, which Russia and Egypt not only abhor, but probably envy. Many of the leaders in both countries openly speak of possibly uniting with each other and becoming independent of the Federation's world currency. How the Prince will deal with this situation, one can only guess. He may not care whatsoever about their plans. The Federation obviously does not need their support in economics. However, Russia is always a military threat with their nuclear weapon capabilities. Because of this, Israel consented to having extra troops brought in to protect the borders from invasion. They even asked the Prince to set up headquarters for himself and Federation troops inside Israel. The Prince also asked for Israel to bring some of its specialized soldiers to the eastern borders for protection. I wonder if the Prince will give up on trying to bring unification to the whole world because of this?

Three Years, Six Months

I can't believe the tragedy I witnessed today. My mind tells me it really happened, but my heart won't believe it. In the last three and a half years since the new beginning, we progressed very close to achieving world peace, but can there ever be peace now? I wonder if the Federation will avenge the death of their beloved leader? Let me begin where I left off at my last writing almost six months ago.

The tensions between Russia, Egypt, Israel, and the Federation mounted toward war. Russia loaded her borders with troops and sent ships into the Mediterranean Sea. Egypt sent troops to its borders ready to invade Israel. The Prince combined with Israel in fortifying both borders. He moved many of his key military personnel into his new headquarters in Israel and then flew into Russia to meet with the Russian leader.

The Prince threatened military action, along with the economic shutdown of their country. He laid down his plans for obtaining all funds from their banks and reserves. He promised to bring Russia to its knees if they persisted in their military maneuvers. He also pointed out that the banking system in Egypt was completely under his control, and he would garnishee all the money from them so that they could not fund any army to ally with Russia. He pointed out that he in no way wanted to fight, but would rather the powers cooperate in unification. He also mentioned that if necessary, he would defend Israel and the rest of the world for the sake of peace.

Immediately following his trip to Russia, he flew into Egypt. He met with the leaders and reiterated the talks in Russia to the Egyptians. He warned them of the severe consequences in fighting Israel and the Federation. He promised them peace and prosperity if they would ally with him and the rest of the world.

Just two days after he left Egypt, they pledged their allegiance to the Federation and world peace. Russia withdrew its troops from the border, though not joining with the Federation. Peace again reigned upon our planet. However, it was short-lived!

Three months after the withdrawal of the Russian troops, China and India voiced their displeasure with the Prince's foreign policies. Both countries were experiencing starvation worse than ever before. They did not feel the Prince's strategies benefited them in any way. They wanted the abundant food in Israel and throughout the Federation to be shared equally. They stirred up many countries from the Far East and even provoked Russia into alliance. Reports filtered in on the westward movement of troops throughout these countries.

About three weeks ago, the Prince made a stunning address to the people of the world:

"The Russians and the Chinese refuse to cooperate with the rest of the world in unification. They insist on wanting to fight and bring war to an otherwise peaceful planet. If they want to bring war to our nations, war is what they shall receive, but I will bring it into their countries instead of ours! With Israel on our side, we have the greatest oil supply in the world. At this moment, Federation ships have blockaded the Persian Gulf and what remains of the Saudi Arabian oil reserves. All nations have been requested to withdraw relations and any supplies from the countries opposing unification. All merchants from the opposed nations are safe in the great city of Babylon, but will not be allowed to leave their sections until their countries agree to peace.

To the Russians, Chinese, and their allies, I say surrender now and work with me in solving the problems we face. If you do not, you will feel the wrath of the Federation and the world. I will wipe you off the map. I will destroy your families, governments, and lands. I will not tolerate your blatant opposition to peace and unification any longer. Prepare yourselves for the onslaught."

I could not believe the fierceness with which he spoke. And who would blame him? Would you sit around while great armies prepared to invade your own nation? He gave them more opportunities to solve the problems peacefully than I would have. Most of the world gave support to the Prince and his actions.

The next day, thousands of Federation paratroopers landed in Poland, Rumania, and Afghanistan. War ships moved into the Arabian Sea and the Straits of Gibraltar. Other countries dispatched their troops to aid the Federation. Israeli fighter jets bombarded several air strips in Russia. What was supposed to be an offensive tactic by the Russians and Chinese became defensive instead.

Within days, millions of troops from around the world reached the borders of Russia, China, and India. Israel supplied the oil and food resources for any country sending military aid. Federation troops and ships blocked all Saudi Arabian oil from reaching the opposed allies. The Israeli and Federation bombers prepared for an onslaught as the first means of invasion.

Before the invasion occurred, the opposed allies surrendered to the Federation for the sake of not destroying their lands. The Prince, along with thousands of troops, flew into Moscow for the official treaty. The invasion fleet, waiting for any sign of hostility, would begin immediately if needed.

In an unusual maneuver, the troops arriving with the Prince sprinted off the planes carrying machine guns, and surrounded the Russian military leaders. Hundreds of bombers and fighter jets flew over Moscow, circling and waiting for the outcome. The Russian troops, somewhat confused by the commotion and probably not prepared for any fighting, surrendered their weapons to the Federation. Instead of delegates walking off the plane, rocket launchers and bazookas were brought out and pointed in every direction.

The troops gathered the Russian heads of state together. They demanded that all Russian troops surrender their weapons or Moscow would be destroyed immediately by the planes circling overhead. With no choice, the Russians dropped their guns and unloaded the artillery. Federation troops swarmed the borders and captured the Russian defense posts. Finally, they marched into Red Square and took over the government buildings. In the same manner, and approximately at the same time, the Federation seized New Delhi and Peking, the capitals of India and China.

The following day, after the opposed countries fell into Federation control, the Prince broadcasted across the world via satellite:

"The world is in a state of peace." (Cheers from the crowd lasted several minutes.) "No blood will be shed by the leaders of Russia, China, or India" (some boos at this point). "We obtained our goal of worldwide peace, thanks to the combined efforts of all involved. The Federation will continue controlling Russia, China, and India until we feel they can coexist with us in total peace" (even louder cheers than before). "Because of this great day in the history of our planet, I am declaring tomorrow as a World Peace holiday!" (The crowd roared with approval.)

I rejoiced with the crowd. Finally, I thought, the world rests from all wars, and even the threat of war! We could now focus upon other pressing problems. With the Prince leading the way, our Utopia would be just around the corner! Or, so I thought.

We celebrated our first World Peace holiday five days ago, just one day after the announcement. The Prince had worked for almost three and a half years since the new beginning to reach this plateau. Why was he not able to enjoy it any longer?

This morning, the Prince held a news conference at the Vatican with the pope. Hundreds of thousands gathered to listen to his latest words of wisdom. Hundreds of millions more watched via satellite from their own homes. He stood behind the podium, confident and happy, speaking of our unification. His hands held the podium like a man with a mission still left undone. The crowd cheered and clapped upon every finished sentence.

No one noticed the man dressed in World Church garb quickly approach from behind. Several Palatine Guards (personal body guards for the World Church) jumped just as the man reached the Prince. He grabbed the Prince's right shoulder from behind and thrust a dagger deep into his back and up into his heart. The Palatine Guards tackled the man and swarmed over the Prince's body like bees on honey. (The crowd went into hysteria and several people died in the pushing and shoving that resulted.)

They rushed the Prince to the hospital, but he was pronounced dead upon arrival. The man that murdered the Prince had eaten poison immediately before he stabbed the Prince. He died on the way to the police station, leaving everything a mystery as to who was behind the assassination. They announced the Prince's funeral in two days and declared it a World Day of Mourning. No business would be allowed to operate.

I still sit here, unable to fully comprehend the Prince's death. My wife cried all afternoon and this evening before she went to bed. She thinks that without the Prince we have no hope for world peace. I tend to agree. Who else can stand in his place? Have his motivation? Have his leadership? Have the power? Why did he have to die? On the other hand, his power may have been too much for anyone to handle. I often thought about how much power he really possessed, and wondered if anyone really understood his control.

Three Days Later

My hands tremble as I write these very words. The last few days will change the course of history, and I witnessed it! For centuries to come, people will wish they could have experienced the excitement, joy, and wonder I felt yesterday.

It all began after the Prince's assassination on Friday. No one knew the fate of the Federation, Russia, China, Israel, or world peace. It seemed every newscaster and politician predicted something different. No one could agree on what would or should follow.

The ten Federation leaders flew into Rome to hold an emergency meeting on Saturday to determine their next course of action. The meetings were held behind closed doors with no media coverage (for obvious reasons). After the meetings on Saturday. they told the media of no immediate plans to change policies or programs already set up by the Prince. When asked about a new leader, they declined to comment on what was discussed.

Sunday morning at eight a.m. (one a.m. our time), the Prince's procession began in Rome. The procession would last for two hours and finish in front of St. Peter's Church in Vatican City. The huge tomb and plaques were prepared all day on Saturday, ready for the burial on Sunday. Because businesses would be closed all day on Sunday, my wife and I decided to stay up and watch the televised event.

The procession held hundreds of cars and military vehicles. The Prince's coffin rested atop a decorated flatbed like one in a parade. It moved at a slow, methodical pace, with millions of mourners jamming the streets. Billions more, like myself, watched from the privacy of their own homes.

All television and radio stations were required to air the

event. Most reviewed film clippings from the last three and a half years of the Prince's rise to dominance. Even I had to admit, the man was undoubtedly the greatest leader of all time. His speeches touched our emotions and his winning personality could melt any heart of stone. His work in bringing peace and unification might never again be matched. The one question that remained was, who would or could take his place?

The procession pulled in front of St. Peter's Church and the coffin neared its destination. The television cameras portrayed the pope and his unusual staid composure. The announcers turned to watch the entrance into the Prince's final resting place. Then it happened! With my own eyes, I noticed the coffin lid move. The Prince's arm thrust the lid open! He sat up and gazed about. The music stopped. The announcers hushed. An eerie silence fell upon the crowd.

The Prince stood up, dressed in his black suit. His voice echoed across the world, "I'm alive! I'm back from the dead!"

He grabbed the suit coat and threw it off his body. His hands found the opening between two buttons on his shirt. He tore the shirt off in similar fashion to the Superman movies of several years back. His exposed chest and back bore the symbol everyone knew. The wound of the sword had healed! It was the Prince himself! The crowds began to cheer and scream. The announcers stammered, "He's alive. That's him. Look at the wound. It's the Prince! He's come back from the dead!"

The guards ran to his vehicle and bowed before him. Hundreds of policemen and military personnel knelt on one knee, chanting, "Hail to the Prince!" The crowds joined in on the chant.

The announcers fumbled for words to say, continuing to repeat their total amazement. One said, "Folks, I don't have words to say. We witnessed the same event and I'm sure you are as stunned as we are."

My wife slid off the couch and onto her knees without taking her eyes off the television set. Her amazement melted into joyfulness. "It's the true King," she mumbled over and over.

The remainder of the day rushed by. The Prince ordered the procession to continue up to his grave. Standing over his tomb, he pronounced his victory over death, with his smile warming the hearts of all who watched. He ordered all countries to follow him for world peace and prosperity, and then called for his private plane, along with several other military jets to accompany him.

He flew into Jerusalem around five p.m. (eight a.m. our time) with ten jets full of his guards and Federation troops. The Israeli government and people welcomed him with open arms. Bands played and thousands of people cheered as he stepped off the plane and began waving to the crowd. Without a word to the crowd that gathered, he stepped into the limousine awaiting his arrival. The troops began pouring into military transports around the Prince's limousine. However, the Prince himself did not travel to the Israeli army headquarters, where a reception was to be held in his honor. Instead, his limousine drove to the newly built temple of the Jews where they performed their sacrifices. Approximately half of his guard followed him, while the other half followed the route to the Israeli headquarters.

The Prince's company halted in front of the temple. His guards rushed out and filled the surrounding area. The Israeli guards, caught by surprise, surrendered their weapons to the Federation troops, who then marched into the outer court of the temple where the priests stood in amazement. They ordered everyone to the side as the Prince stepped out of his limousine and walked into the temple. The troops then moved into the inner court (the holy place) and lined up in the entrance of what the Jewish priests call the Holy of Holies. The Prince strutted toward the curtains covering the opening. The television cameras followed with the other military personnel, picking up the Prince's every move.

The priests began to scream at the Prince about not being

allowed to enter the temple. They warned him of God's judgments upon anyone who entered into the Holy of Holies. At this, the Prince stopped in front of the curtains and turned to face the priests. He grinned in a sly manner, almost wickedly. His eyebrows dropped menacingly, and his head tilted downward as he stared at the high priest with glaring eyes. His grin turned into a smile and he lifted his head without taking his eyes off the high priest. His laugh sounded like one knowing victory was at hand. "I am God!" he said in a powerful, deep voice.

He turned back and firmly grasped the curtains. He yanked them apart and stared at the throne in front of him (the Jews call it the mercy seat). He paused for only a moment before continuing his march up to the throne. He sat down upon it as people filled the room around him. He spoke with a deep, almost inhuman voice. "I am God! I am the great King who was dead and now lives. All will worship me. All will follow me. I am the Messiah, the Savior of mankind. You will worship no other god, but me. I am the Christ!"

His words echoed deep within me. Down to my heart I could feel the tingling sensation begin. My entire body shook for a moment with a chill. My wife knelt before the television screen. Her hands lifted high above her head and then lowered in front of her as she chanted, "Praise the King. Praise the Messiah. Praise the King. Praise the Messiah."

The crowd gathered around and knelt down in front of the Prince. They chanted praises to him, while the Prince beamed with glory, reveling in the praises of the crowd. Looking closer, I noticed the lines of determination upon his face, like an unaccomplished task of major proportions lay before him. It was almost as if this was not the pinnacle of glory for him.

I stood up and walked out of the room. My wife did not even notice my departure. I walked out the front door into the refreshing coolness of the morning air. Taking a deep breath, I gazed up at the overcast sky. I started walking down our sidewalk and down the street. The neighborhood seemed unusually still, probably due to everyone being inside watching the Prince.

The excitement, joy, wonder, and I hate to admit, the fear, weighed heavily on my mind. I wanted to be able to fall on my knees and feel the pure excitement my wife and everyone else was experiencing. Why can't I just take things at face value? Why do I always doubt everything? Even though doubts swept through my mind, I did feel some excitement. It's just that all the unanswered questions bother me. If he really is God, what about all these disasters we have been having? Is he the only God? How can I deny the resurrection? I saw it with my own eyes. If that doesn't prove he is God, what will? Who but God could rise from the dead? Then of course, what about Jesus? He supposedly rose from the dead. Is he another God? Did he really rise from the dead? I saw the Prince arise. I never, never saw Jesus do it, and there are so many people who don't believe He really did anyway. What about the disappearance? If the Prince was God, does that mean he took people from earth? But that's impossible. Maybe the Prince is the Christ sent of God to lead us into peace and prosperity. His life, until now, has been built on bringing peace to the world. Maybe God raised him from the dead to prove he was the Christ. Then again, what about the disasters we have been having? Unless . . . they are the testing period before we reach our Utopia!

My conclusions brought a sense of relief as I walked back to the house. I wasn't ready to bow down before the Prince like my wife and probably the rest of the world was, but just the hope of the Prince being the Christ gave possible answers to all my questions.

When I returned home, my wife filled me in on how the Federation easily conquered Israel. Because of the possible wars, extra Federation troops were present throughout all of Israel, paving the way for a quick takeover with no gunfire at all! The Israeli troops were so taken by surprise that they did not even bother to fight. The Federation seized Israel's headquarters at the same time the Prince marched into the temple. The already stationed Federation troops moved with precision to cover the Israeli soldiers when the military vehicles pulled in and out came Federation troops with guns pointing. The surprised Israeli leaders were expecting the Prince, not troops with guns ready to fire. They surrendered without a gunshot.

One thing is sure: whether or not the Prince is God, he now controls the world. After his resurrection, no one in the Federation will dare to oppose him. China, Russia, India, and now Israel are under his command. There is nothing left for him to conquer.

Eight Days Later

The first catastrophe in months descended two nights ago, just three days after the Prince's resurrection and continued until three yesterday afternoon. All of yesterday and most of today, I spent fighting the fires and protecting my house. I did not sleep a wink last night due to all the fires. I finally relaxed and took a nap about five today. My wife woke me up around ten, in time for the news and dinner. I returned to my bed, but I couldn't sleep and decided to write down all that happened.

It began around two in the morning. I woke up suddenly when a lightning bolt hit right outside our house and hail began to pound on our roof. The light from our digital clock went out, showing the power failure. I reassured my wife that everything was okay and I walked over to the window. To my horror, one of our oak trees had split down the middle and was burning like a torch. Another bolt of lightning flashed in front of my eyes and knocked me backward onto the floor. Slowly crawling to the window, I peered out from on my knees.

The hail plummeted down from the sky, with the largest chunks ranging from golf ball to tennis ball size. To my amazement, the ground was not covered with hail. As hard as it was coming down, I thought surely the ground would be covered like snow, but it wasn't. From the light of the fire, I noticed a dark liquid under the oak tree, not like water from hail melting, but a colored, thicker liquid. I squinted my eyes and pressed against the window to identify the unusual substance. Again, a bolt of lightning struck close by, knocking me to the floor. The bright flash blinded me for several minutes. My wife jumped out of bed and crawled over to me. I told her I was fine and asked her to see if she could identify the liquid. She vehemently opposed going near the window, and tried to persuade me to come back to bed until the storm passed.

After my eyes adjusted, I stood up and walked over to the bedroom door. I told my wife that I needed to make sure everything was all right with the house. Stumbling in the dark, I felt through the hallway into the kitchen. After I opened the pantry door, another flash of lightning illuminated the room, allowing me to find the flashlight in the usual place. To my delight, it actually worked!

I walked toward the front door. The continual sound of the hail pounding the roof and the deafening thunder did not even phase me. Nor did the bright flashes of light frighten me. My curiosity about that liquid drove me not to heed any warnings of danger. I just had to know what it was.

I reached the front door just as another lightning bolt struck nearby. It was then that I first noticed the rain coming down with the hail. Opening the front door, I stepped onto the porch. The hail hitting the roof echoed twice as loud outside as it did inside the house. The warmth hit me like walking into a furnace room. It had to be in the eighties. That would explain why the hail did not accumulate on the ground, but how in the world could it be hailing when it was this warm to begin with?

My flashlight shone onto the dark, reddish liquid covering the sidewalk. I walked to the edge of the porch and knelt down. My hand quivered as I touched the liquid and brought it up to my face. Slowly dropping my hand, I lifted my head to the sky. Blood! My body convulsed with a shiver. Impossible. Blood? From the sky?

Hoping to shake it off, I shook my hand violently. I ran back inside and went to the kitchen sink. As I washed my hands and face, my mind raced with all the possibilities. Nothing could explain this horror. It had to be from God. But, why?

My thoughts were interrupted by a low wailing sound.

The emergency siren gradually reached an ear-piercing whistle. My wife screamed for me. I dried my face and went back into the bedroom. My wife held our children in her arms and inundated me with questions that I brushed off.

How can one explain… blood? I knew she would get even more upset at the mere thought of blood all over our house and yard. We cuddled and comforted our kids and I told them to get some sleep while the storm passed over. However, no one could sleep with the flashes of lightning and the sounds of sirens, thunder. and hail crashing all around. Instead, we lay in bed wondering when it would stop, hoping that no major damage would occur. Yet, I knew. No way would a storm like this just pass by without major damage. The question was not if there would be damage, but how much. I sat there quietly, not being able to sleep, pondering the events thus far.

It must have been around five in the morning, while I was trying to figure out how in the world it could be so warm and still have a hailstorm, when an orange glow shone into the bedroom window. I sat up. My wife clung to me for a moment, but let go. Stepping over to the window, I peered out into the yard. Fire! The trees, grass, and bushes all blazed in an orange fury.

Instinctively, I ran to the closet, groping for some jeans and a flannel shirt. My wife ran to the window and stared in amazement. I found my leather work boots and struggled to lace them up in the dark, while my wife calmly walked over to the closet and began dressing in old clothes. I asked her if she was okay. She explained in a calm voice that we had to protect the house and something told me not to interfere with her wishes of wanting to help.

After lacing my boots, I ran out onto the porch. Our entire yard burned in an orange flame! Our bushes, the garden, and the trees crackled like a new log when it is thrown onto a fire. I looked around our house to see if the fire had spread to it. Luckily, it hadn't. I ran along the blood-covered sidewalk toward the garden hose, with hail pelting me like somebody dropping marbles. Then a golf ball-sized one landed on top of my head. Shaking my head in pain, I ran back inside to get some covering.

My wife met me at the door with a puzzled look. For a moment, she stared inquisitively at the liquid covering my body, then her eyes widened as big as a half dollar. She mumbled something about blood and took a few steps back. Her screams pierced my ears as I started toward her. My outstretched arms dripped with blood, as she ran from me like I was the plague or a killer. I had forgotten to warn her about the blood. Oh, well, no time to comfort or explain now. The house had to be saved.

I went to the front closet and grabbed two hats. Hesitating for a moment, I slipped on my rain coat. It would be hot, but I needed protection from the hail. I also found some heavy work gloves and slipped them over my hands. My wife sobbed in the bedroom as I ran out the front door.

I made it to the hose and began squirting the grass. The water had no effect on the fire. Throwing down the hose in disgust, I ran around to check the rest of the house. To my relief, the fire seemed to be stopping at the edge of the grass. After checking all around the house, I ran back into the garage and grabbed a couple of shovels and a pick. I went back outside and began digging into the fiery ground, covering the grass with dirt. My hope mounted as the fire didn't spread onto the dirt, which in turn protected the house. I still worried about a lightning bolt hitting, but it never occurred.

As I worked through the day, I avoided looking up. Not only would the hail smash my face, but the blood would pour into my eyes, ears, nose, and mouth. It tasted and smelled disgusting. My eyes watered from the irritation and I rubbed them continually. Later, after it stopped, the blood hardened on whatever it touched. My clothes, my skin, my hair, the ground, the house, everything was covered with dried blood. It nauseates me now even thinking about the stench. The only reason I did not get sick during the storm was because of my involvement with protecting my house and others' gave me no time to think about how disgusting the blood was.

Finally, I finished the digging around two and went inside, where my wife prepared a lunch for me. She acted very strange, almost as if nothing was wrong. She gabbed about the neighbors and things needing to get done, but she would not touch me, because of the blood covering my clothes.

Around three in the afternoon I heard a couple of loud thunderclaps. The hail came down even harder than before, and a multitude of lightning bolts flashed all around. Then it all stopped. I ran outside to see the clouds roll back and reveal the sun. Basking in the sunlight, I felt a sense of relief rush through me. The crackling of fire interrupted my brief repose, as I saw my neighbors battling their house fires. The rest of the day and night was spent fighting the fires throughout the neighborhood.

The devastation was unbelievable. Only a few trees remained standing. Green grass or shrubbery could not be found anywhere. Many homes were partially damaged by the fires, while others lost everything. The entire water supply was virtually exhausted. Fortunately, though, someone with his head on straight shut off the waterworks so we would have drinking water later. The remaining water is being rationed and regulated on its daily use. No baths or showers are allowed… just enough to get a wash cloth wet and clean ourselves with soap. The electricity came on around seven this evening. By the time I woke up, everything seemed to be calmed down.

The news said that the storm was worldwide! They showed reports from Europe, Africa, Russia, and the United States. The approximate damages are believed to be in the trillions of dollars. Approximately one-third of our forests and all green grass was destroyed! The few trees left in the U.S. were saved by the rains that followed after the storm. The rains quenched most of the fires that were still raging.

It rained here beginning around ten this evening. The slow methodical sound of rain on our house relieved my wife greatly. She fell asleep soon after it started. I went outside to feel the real water this time. The cool, clean drops smacked my face and trickled down my chin. My lips opened to taste each refreshing drop. It felt so good and reassuring that I stood outside for almost ten minutes as the rain soaked through to my skin.

Three Years, Seven Months

In only one month since his resurrection, the King has managed to turn the world completely upside-down in following and worshipping him. The World Church was dissolved and all the assets seized by the Federation kings. The pope pledged his allegiance to the King, and is now his right-hand man. In political matters, the world was saved from economic ruin, thanks to the mastery of the King.

The fires resulted in the bankruptcy of every fire insurance company in the world. Within one week, homeowners and businesses claimed over one trillion dollars in losses! The insurance companies could cover only a small portion of the damages. When the millions of claims rolled in, they had no other alternative than to declare bankruptcy, leaving hundreds of millions of people around the world homeless and in the streets. Every motel and hotel filled up in two days as people found shelter. Making matters worse, many businesses closed down from extreme damage to their buildings and property. When the insurance companies folded, no funds were available to refurbish the buildings and restore them to operating order. Thus, many businesses closed and dismissed their workers permanently. As one could imagine, the economy quickly spiraled downward.

In a brilliant economic maneuver by the King, he ordered the insurance companies to pay a percentage on all claims. They would use all their liquid assets (minus operating expenses) in partial payment of each claim. The greatest percentage was to be given to any company that would reopen and return workers to their jobs. A much smaller percentage was reserved for homeowners in order for them to survive somewhere. No money would be given to any company not re-opening. This stabilized the economy not only in our nation, but across the globe. However, since my government division deals with economics, I have been working eighty to ninety hours a week keeping up with the regulations and the enforcement of the new laws. I am not complaining, though. At least I have a job and a good salary.

On the religious front, the World Church is being abolished. With everyone worshipping the King as God, there is no need to have the World Church. With that in mind, the ten Federation kings implemented a plan to raze all church buildings and recover all the riches from each church. The King approved their plan and promised complete military support, if needed. They began this week by taking over the Vatican, ordering all priests and spiritual leaders to report to them for new assignments in worshipping the King.

If you are wondering what happened to the pope, his story is almost as exciting as the King's! A week after the big storm and fires, the pope arrived in Jerusalem. It was the first meeting of the two since he left Rome the day of the King's resurrection. Hundreds of thousands gathered in the streets to see the pope as the procession passed from the airport to the temple. Every station broadcasted the entrance of the pope into the temple. All watched with anticipation of what he would say and do in front of the self-proclaimed God, the King.

The pope sauntered through the entrance and up to the King. The King stood up majestically from his throne as the pope stopped in front of him. They gazed at each other with an unusual friendliness. The King's face never changed from his blank expression, but I noticed his head tilt slightly back and to the side as if approving the time of a premeditated response. The pope fell to his knees and did obeisance to the King. "The Messiah is come! All must worship the King, our Savior!"

He ordered the guards to bring up a lamb and put it on the altar in front of the temple. He stepped back to allow the King to pass in front of him and then bowed, stretching his arm to point the way for the King. The King stepped down and strolled past the pope and through the curtains. The pope followed close behind. They stood in front of the altar as the lamb was tied down. The pope again commanded all people to worship the King as he lifted up his hands to heaven. He tilted his head back and closed his eyes. Within seconds, a column of fire quickly descended from the sky, engulfing the altar and devouring the lamb. Everyone around the pope and King fell to their faces and gave praise to the King and the great prophet who could bring fire from heaven.

The pope then told anyone with a disease or sickness to come before him. After a minute of stillness and silence, a man limped up to the pope. He told the popc of his dislocated hip from birth that surgery could not fix. The pope took his hand and hit the man's hip. Hc immediately stood upright and jumped around in front of the King and pope, giving praises to them. The pope ordered him to give praise only to the King. Many more came before the pope that day, with diseases and sicknesses to be healed. He cured them all in the sight of the King.

The next day, the pope began work on his plans to glorify the King. He ordered top scientists and technicians to develop an android in the likeness of the King. He also gave other top secret orders dealing with some type of hologram and the use of television and computers. He would not disclose the entire project to the public until it was finished. Today, the pope revealed his finished work for the first time.

Every television station broadcasted from the temple as the pope spoke of the great new creation. He stepped back from the microphones and pulled the sheets off to unveil the nine-foot-tall android that was an exact representation of the King. The audience clapped and praised the work of the pope. The King smiled and gave his approval to him.

The pope just smiled as the android's eyes opened. The audience gasped when the android spoke in a deep tone, matching the King's voice. "You will worship me. I am the great King. I have risen from the dead. Bow down before me."

The android moved in slow, but fluent motion toward the King. The King smirked in approval without showing the least bit of fear as the giant stepped toward him. It stepped up next to the King and turned back to the crowd. "Fall down before me or die!" it commanded.

The guards immediately fell to their knees before the android and almost everyone followed. A few reporters continued jotting notes without heeding the warning of the giant. His eyes fixed upon the closest reporter jotting notes. The reporter stopped writing and looked up with puzzlement toward the android. He dropped his paper and pen and clutched his chest with both hands. He did not even gasp while falling to the floor. The android fixed his eyes upon the next reporter, and the next. Each one clutched his chest in similar fashion, sprawling to the floor face first before him. His words echoed louder than before, "Fall down and worship me, or die!"

The pope stepped back to the microphones. "Tomorrow at noon, all will worship the King and his image. Please tune in your televisions to any channel for the broadcast. The King demands all citizens of the world unite in worship, in order to bring in our new age."

I turned off the television and looked at my wife. She stared in amazement at the blank screen. "Wow, is that awesome or what?" she asked.

"I have to admit," I replied, "the technology in that piece of machinery is incredible, but did you notice what happened to those reporters in the room? What did the android do?"

"I don't know, did they die?" she questioned.

"I'm sure of it. But, how? Or, why?"

"I don't know, but I'm going to make sure to tune in tomorrow at noon and you can bet I'll worship the King!" she proclaimed with assurance.

I questioned whether I would or not. I still did not have

the same commitment my wife seemed to have for the King. I greatly respect the King and he definitely is a god. Only a god could raise himself from the dead. My mind urges me to trust the King, but deep down in my heart, something doesn't seem right. I can't put my finger on it. Why do I not have peace about worshipping the King as God?

The King himself spoke about another God, the God of the Jews. He claims the God of the Jews brought the great storm and fires. He says we must kill all Jews if we ever want to be completely free of the evil events happening on earth. He ordered the execution of every Jew in any country. The Federation troops mowed down hundreds at a time with their machine guns in the streets of Jerusalem and throughout Israel immediately after the King's proclamation. Millions have been killed already this month, and the Federation troops are in hot pursuit of a band moving into the wilderness.

I could not sleep last night thinking about the android and replaying how he gazed upon the reporters. Tossing and turning in bed, I imagined those eyes fixed upon me. The world has no choice. They must worship the King and his image. I didn't appreciate the idea of no choice in the matter. Why was it necessary to actually worship him? What difference would it make if we didn't? If worse came to worst, I could pretend to worship him without actually doing it. Who would know?

The Next Day

After tossing and turning all night, I finally managed to drag myself out of bed around six. All I could think about was the telecast at noon. Over and over, my mind played out the different ways I could fake my worship of the King and his android. I would play it cool and watch what everyone else did. Maybe there would be others like myself that did not want to bow down. Would we end up like the reporters?

My wife bounded out of bed, already talking about the telecast and what a great day it would be. She walked briskly by me and into our closet, gathering her clothes for the day. I leaned up against the door post, watching her for a moment. I would like to say her cheerfulness and exuberance brought new life to me, but it didn't. Between not having slept and my uncertainty of the telecast, I disdained her carefree attitude. Clothes slung over her arm, she came out and kissed me on the cheek while passing on to the bathroom. She really is a good wife, even if she is a morning person.

After my morning shower and shave, I walked to the breakfast table in a little better mood. The scent of bacon and eggs caught my nostrils. My eyes opened a tad bit more with the anticipation of a hearty meal. My daughter sat in her high chair, playing with her dry cereal. I walked up to my wife and gave her a hug from behind, as she patted the back of my head with her hand. Sitting down next to my daughter, I began playing with the cereal in front of her. My son watched from the side and his laughter lifted my spirits even more. My wife scolded me for distracting her from finishing breakfast, and I gave her one of my "Who, me?" looks. She shook her head and said, "You're just an overgrown kid."

Recalling the fulfillment of my morning's breakfast, I left

for work. Thoughts about our family and how happy we were eased my apprehensions for what was about to take place. Nothing soothes the soul like playing with your own kids in the morning and eating with your wife as the sun shines through the window. I felt refreshed and relieved. My night of dread that seemed to linger on forever was long forgotten. Parking in my reserved space, I walked up to the office door. Whatever it would take to keep my family together and make us happy, I would do.

The office buzzed with excitement over the upcoming broadcast. Some people doubted the idea of worshipping the King. Feeling just like me, they too questioned why we should be forced to worship him if we didn't want to. When I asked several of the doubters if they were going to bow down in worship, they all said they probably would just for the sake of not causing problems, as well as for not wanting to die.

By far, the greatest majority of employees looked forward to the telecast with excitement and joy. They all acted just like my wife, chattering about how awesome the King is and how he would save the world. They talked about his resurrection and the android. Everyone felt the pope's miracles and his support of the King were the final proof of his deity.

Throughout the morning I struggled with my thoughts and feelings. I was happy to hear there were at least a few that doubted, like myself. At least I wasn't completely alone. However, sooner or later I would need to make a decision. If the King isn't the Messiah, the world is doomed. If he is the Messiah, though, I want to worship him to ensure my safety and place in the new world. After much debate, I decided to watch and see if everyone else bowed down and then I would follow if needed, even though my heart would not be in it.

At eleven thirty, I made the announcement for all to gather in the lunchroom. Being a government office, we were required to set up a large-screen television for viewing. One of the spiritual guides from the old World Church (now a representative for the King and the pope) stood in the back of the room with paper and pencil in hand. He planned to write down anyone who would not worship. He stopped me and asked if I would allow him a moment to speak before the telecast began. "No problem. Whatever I can do to help you and the King would be my pleasure," I answered.

My politeness surprised even me. I wanted to make sure to at least look like I was fully behind the King. It never hurts to brown-nose the powers at hand. The guide nodded his approval and thanked me for my cooperation.

I addressed the crowd and asked them to quiet down, while reminding all managers to hand in their lists of attendance (if someone failed to attend, that person would automatically be fired). Introducing the guide, I went to the back of the room to observe the event. He asked everyone to spread out and allow enough room in front for prostration. He explained the pope's new law that would result in death if not obeyed. He turned to the television and switched it on. Moving out of the way, he walked back to the doorway about forty feet from me.

We tuned in just as the station switched to Jerusalem. The pope addressed the camera and proclaimed this the greatest day in the history of world peace. All people of every race and nationality would unite today in the worship of the Messiah. We must now bow in worship to the King and his image.

With that, the screen blacked out and drums began playing faintly in the background. The sound reminded me of some type of tribal music from Africa. It grew louder and louder with several flutes joining in to blend with the drums. Various other instruments joined in to produce a beautiful, mellowing sound. I felt myself swaying back and forth, not wanting to stop. As I stared into the blank screen, voices softly chanted, blending into the music.

Suddenly, in a split second, he stood before me. The King towered above me, staring down into my eyes. His nine-foot frame filled the room with power. He held a shield in one hand and a sword .in the other. His hand clutched the sword in a death grip as he raised it into the air. The light from his presence shone throughout the room and I looked down while closing my eyes from the brightness.

The deep, commanding voice slowly started, "I am the King who was wounded from the sword, but now I live!"

I fell to my knees without daring to look up.

The voice grew stronger and deeper, "You will bow down and worship me. You will serve no other God. Worship me! I am God!"

I bowed down and my head touched the floor. Others around the room began lifting their voices in praise and adoration, "Praise the King. Praise the Messiah. Praise his name."

The voice continued with strength, urgency, and more power, "Those who will not follow me will die! Worship me and live! I am the King!"

The words echoed as the King disappeared from the room. The music softened and the chanting ceased. Opening my eyes, I glanced around the room. Others lifted themselves and rubbed their eyes. Standing up, I walked out of the room without a word to anyone. While walking back to my office, I listened to the laudation and wonderment of the other employees from the hallway. The glory and power of the image awed even me.

Later in the afternoon, I listened to the news on the radio. The pope announced the need to be identified with the King. All people of the world must show their allegiance to the King and world unity by receiving an identification mark on either their right hand or forehead. In one month, only those with identification could buy or sell any goods. Anyone without the mark would be considered a threat to world unity as well as to the King and would be executed.

I returned home to an enthusiastic wife explaining the image that came right into our own living room from the television. She wondered, with great admiration, about the wisdom and knowledge of our King. Her joyfulness extended to our daughter, who proudly pronounced her new word, "Messiah."

Smiling to my daughter, I walked into my study to think. Somewhere before, I had heard about the identification symbol. At least, I thought I had. Maybe it was *deja vu.* Yet, with all the great and wonderful things happening, deep down inside I could feel something wrong about this new symbol. I just couldn't put my finger on it.

Three Years, Eight Months

Today was the deadline to receive the Unification Symbol. For the last month, billions and billions of people lined up at processing centers to receive the symbol. The first day, over two hundred million people pledged their allegiance to the King by acquiring one of the three unification tattoos: his name, his image, or a computer insignia that supposedly contains a number identification of his name. Even with the speed of the machines, the centers could not keep up with the crowds that gathered. Newscasts viewed the hours-long lines at various centers around our town. The people they interviewed waiting in line all spoke with gladness and appreciation of the King. Everyone wanted to show their allegiance to him by receiving his symbol permanently. Several mentioned wanting to avoid the huge lines that might occur from those postponing until the deadline.

As the deadline approached, the rules became more specific on the Unified Symbol. The pope informed the world that those not receiving the symbol would be questioned and asked to worship the King or his image. If they bowed and worshipped, they would be set free, but would still not be allowed to buy or sell anything until they received the symbol. If they would not bow before the image, they would be executed by the guillotine. All merchants would be required to report the name of anyone attempting to buy from them without the Unified Symbol. To receive a license, all merchants must show their Unified Symbol.

My wife and I argued several times concerning the symbol. She received the image symbol the first day the processing centers were opened. Our son received his at school during the first week. Neither understood my apprehensions about receiving something so permanent on my hand or forehead. She became rather upset and called me a traitor to the King. I pointed out my obeisance to the image, but she continued her accusations of my disloyalty. She threatened to move out and take the kids with her if I did not receive the symbol by the deadline. She refused to be associated with someone who was known as a rebel.

I could not get over my fearfulness of receiving a permanent mark. I truly wanted to follow the King, but my stomach turned inside me at the thought of a permanent mark upon my hand. Could it be the nervousness of making a real commitment, much like the day I stood on the altar and committed myself to my wife? Even though it was the best thing to do, I couldn't help but think I might be making a big mistake. Every possible rational explanation of backing out flashed through my mind as I walked down the aisle, but I pledged my love to her anyway. Afterward, I was grateful and thankful for my commitment. The same nervousness swept over me as I thought about pledging myself to the King.

The final day came. My wife, who would barely talk to me, asked if I was going to get it done. I said I would during lunch today. She brightened up, hugged me, and talked about how happy we were going to be. My son asked, "Are you finally going to pledge your allegiance to the King?"

"Yes, son", I answered with a smile. I kissed my wife and walked out the door.

On my way to work I saw a billboard advertising the Unification Symbol. Six people with determined, but content looks, held their fists tight in front of them, each displaying one of the three symbols: a black man on the left and a white woman in the middle had the King's name; a Chinese woman next to the black man, and a Mexican man bore the image of the King; and an African woman in the middle, and a white man on the right had the numerical computer symbol. Underneath was written, "United we stand."

At that moment, I remembered the conversation in my

office over a year ago, with the young man who died. He warned me about not taking a mark. "Ahhh!" I thought out loud, "that's why I have such a bad feeling about taking the Unified Symbol; all because of the weird guy who refused to join the World Church."

I paused for a moment. How did he know there would be a mark from the King? He knew of the symbol before the Great Prophet revealed the plan; unless, of course, information leaked from the Vatican or the Federation prior to the law. "That must be it," I continued out loud, "the information leaked out early."

After arriving at the office, the harassment continued. Everyone asked why I had not received a symbol. (I was the only one left in our building who did not have it.) I assured everyone that I had been too busy to get it done any sooner and would be going down today at lunch. My boss in Washington even called to make sure that everyone in the entire office wore the symbol. He told me to fire anyone who did not follow along with the King's orders. "Not to worry," I told him, "the last ones are going today to get it done."

At lunch time, I left for a center about three blocks from my office. Walking at an unusually slow pace, I contemplated my situation. The logical choice was to receive the mark and be done with it, but that uneasy feeling upset my stomach. Could I just ignore these feelings? I decided to rationally think out all the possibilities in my own mind.

Why would I not do it? Because of my upset stomach, my nervousness, or the fanatical young man? Or was it simply because of the commitment to the King for the rest of my life?

Now, why should I do it? To survive. Because my wife would leave me. To survive. Our family would break up. To survive. To keep my job. To survive. To go along with the rest of the world. To survive. So I would not have to live off the land without a single friend. To survive. Because the King deserves our allegiance for all he's done for us. To survive.

Because the King is our Savior. To survive.

There was no doubt, for survival's sake, I needed to receive the symbol of the King. Only an idiot would go off into the land when all he had to do was receive a mark on the hand or forehead. Logically, I would be grateful and thankful, once it was done.

As my pace quickened, I began to think about what the King had done for us. Not only has he given us answers for world problems, but he has also brought world peace for the first time in history. The Great Prophet performs miracles and proclaims him as the Messiah, and above all, he raised himself from the dead to prove he was God! How can anyone deny it?

I reached the center where hundreds stood in line. All of them were discussing the King and the pope. I overheard several talking about their doubts, but all decided the logical choice was to receive the symbol. Others talked about the great glories of the King and his rise to fame.

My thoughts were interrupted by a low voice behind me. "Why did you wait so long?"

I turned around to a muscular man looking down at me. His scraggly, dirty brown beard reached down to his massive chest. His long, straight hair was pulled back in a ponytail off his face. Old overalls covered his large frame and flannel shirt filled with holes. "Excuse me?" I answered.

"How come you waited so long to receive the symbol?" he questioned again.

"I'm not sure. I guess I've had a lot of doubts. Yourself?."

"I ran off into the country when I heard about the symbol. Someone warned me not to take it a couple years back."

"Same with me," I interrupted.

He continued as if he did not hear me. "I tried to make it out in the wild, but couldn't do it. I finally found my way back into the city and realized the best thing to do was follow the King if I wanted to survive."

"Yeah, me, too," another man said, breaking into the conversation. "Somebody warned me a year ago about not taking the symbol, so I've been having doubts about doing it until now."

"Wht did you change your mind?" I asked.

"I want to survive!"

Others joined in on our conversation as we stood in line. Feelings seemed mutual as just about everyone expressed doubts and fears about taking the symbol. I was greatly encouraged by their openness with each other. We concluded that our only chance of survival hung on the decision to receive the mark.

The time flew by and before I knew it, I was through the doors and next in line. I listened as they asked the one in front of me what symbol she wanted and whether she preferred it on her hand or forehead. She chose the King's name and asked for it on her forehead. She stood there for a moment as they lifted the machine above her eyes. A buzz came from the machine and they thanked her for having it done.

I stood in front of the three officers. Each one portrayed a form of confidence and coldness. I felt like a cow being led to the slaughter, a piece of meat stamped for possession. Their eyes glazed over with numbness, like the men who shock the cows before they die. Their hands felt ice cold, as with no feeling, while they grabbed me on my arm to bring me forward.

"Which symbol do you want?" one asked.

"Uhh, uhh, the name," I stuttered.

"Forehead or right hand?" another asked in a slow monotone voice, similar to that of a robot running out of juice.

"Uhh, uhh, hand," I squeaked softly.

The robot officer took my hand with his ice-cold claws. He wiped my hand with a wet cloth smelling of disinfectant. He then placed my shaking hand onto the table. The third officer brought the machine over, slowly dropping it onto the back of my cold hand. I felt a tingling sensation run through my arm and down my spine.

Three Years, Nine Months

An odd event took place on my way to work yesterday. I was sitting at a stoplight, not paying attention to anything in particular, when a bright flash blinded my eyes. I dropped down beneath my dash, thinking that a nuclear warhead had exploded. My car continued running though, and there was no static in the radio as if a real nuclear weapon had detonated. My eyes slowly regained sight, as if recovering from the momentary blindness of a camera flash. By then, the horns started to blast from a combination of people stopped in the middle of the road and a few minor accidents.

Upon arrival at work, I was greeted by my secretary as she rushed up to me with the latest report. "Sir, Washington called just a few moments ago. They want you to fly to New York immediately!"

Calling back to Washington, I found out the damage from the flash of light. Apparently, large parts of the oceans and seas have become blood! Outside of New York, the entire Long Island Sound, New York Bay, and hundreds of miles of the Atlantic Ocean have turned to blood. They wanted me and three other economic advisors to examine the area and assess the damage.

Washington had already called and set up a plane ticket on the earliest flight available, so I hopped into a taxi and rushed to the airport. I arrived in New York City around one p.m., and they had a helicopter waiting for me with another of the economic advisors inside. The helicopter flew us over New York Bay, Long Island Sound, and over the Atlantic Ocean. The sight was repulsive. Everywhere I looked, dead marine animals were floating on top of the blood. Every ship in the ports was either turned upside down or sunk with only a small portion of the hull above the blood. We flew out over the ocean about fifty miles, and as far as we could see, the once-blue ocean waters had been changed to the horrid sight of blood and dead fish. My eyes watered as we passed over a herd of whales turned upside-down in the sea. The pilot informed us that every ship caught in the blood had sunk. No survivors have been found from any ship except those in port where crew members jumped onto the docks.

The four of us spent last night and today in a hotel, listening to the news reports, and discussing possible economic solutions. The news reported that one-third of all seas and oceans around the world had become blood, causing every ship to be destroyed and every fish to die. No one had any explanation for the phenomenon except the King. He blames the God of the Jews for doing this to us, and has strengthened his efforts to eliminate all Jews from the face of the earth (those who claim Jesus is Messiah instead of our King). All this on the heels of the King's new Bill of Commandments, which became law about a week ago.

The Bill of Commandments changes many previously held beliefs and upholds the deity of the King. The first commandment requires the worship of him or his image. Those failing to do so will be put to death by the guillotine. This law reinforces the previous law made by the pope.

The second commandment requires all homes to have a replica of the King to worship. Wood, gold, silver, or any metal can be used for the prototype. The third commandment upholds the freedom of speech. No word will be considered vulgar and we are all free to say whatever we please, including slanderous remarks.

The fourth commandment allows all businesses to be open seven days a week, basically annulling the once-held belief of having Sunday as a holy day. This allows all businesses and people to do as they please and make as much money as they want.

The fifth commandment releases children from the bondage of the parent. The parents are not required to provide for any child, nor the children for their parents. Any child turning in a parent for disobeying one of the King's commandments would be protected by the King's force.

The sixth commandment allows the killing of someone for breaking a commandment or for revenge. In other words, if someone breaks a commandment, that person may be put to death by anyone. If one feels he has been wronged, he may kill the person who wronged him. Of course, it also allows one to kill in self-defense.

The seventh commandment annuls the institution of marriage. One may choose to be with whomever one wishes. If one chooses to continue living with his or her partner, one may do so. However, no one is under commitment to abstain from anyone else if one wants. In other words, we may now have free love without repercussions.

The eighth commandment allows for stealing when necessary. People who cannot meet a debt, may take whatever they wish. However, anyone who catches the thief stealing one's own possession may do as he or she pleases to the thief.

The ninth commandment regards lying as a means to avoid punishment or for personal gain. If one needs to lie to avoid being killed by another, he or she may do so with no guilt. Plus, in dealings of business, a lie is considered part of the trading game. Each businessman should know enough not to be taken in by a lie. If some lose out because of gullibility, that is their problem.

The tenth and final commandment frees our conscience from wanting more than we have. Basically, we may desire anything from our neighbor and go for it if we want. If our neighbor's live-in partner looks good to us, we may have free love. If his car or house is better, we may freely desire to have them without guilt. However, the previous nine commandments will apply.

The King's Bill of Commandments is heralded by many as the free society we have always desired. Whatever our hearts yearn for can no longer be withheld. There will be no more guilt or bad feelings over doing what we truly desire. No one will be able to push personal beliefs on anyone. For the first time in history, we can enjoy as much personal pleasure as we want!

The Book of the King outlines all leaders' responsibilities to the King and their powers. The smallest details of taxing (or offerings, as the King calls it) are set out. Each leader's freedom of reign is written out so as not to cause any problems with the King. Of course, no one knows exactly what is in it, for only the King and the leaders are allowed to read it, but we are to obey the leaders as we would the King.

The greatest achievement of the law comes from the elimination of the court system. No courts are needed to resolve conflicts between anyone. The Bill of Commandments outlines all we need to live in peace with one another. From India to Russia, the United States to Africa, we now all live under the same laws. If by chance something could possibly arise that is not covered, they may ask to plead their case with the leader of the region. The leader's word is final and will be upheld by the King's force.

My wife (live-in partner; I still have a hard time not calling her my wife) and I sat down for a talk after the new laws came into effect. She agreed with me that we got along well and wanted to continue living together. However, there were a couple of men at the office where she works that she would like to be with once in a while. I thought that was fair, since there were several ladies I wanted to be with as well. We also decided that being open about everything was the most important aspect of our relationship.

I realize now that we are taking our first steps into the new age. Our King is changing laws to allow us the pursuit of happiness and fulfillment. We have no more need to feel bad or guilty in doing what we perceive as the right thing for us. The court system is being eliminated, with our King heading all authority. The world is united in following the King and all nations are at peace with one another for the first time. I am also blessed with a great family and an incredible partner. The only negative involves the Jews and Christians left on earth. Will their God leave us alone if we eliminate all of his people?

Four Years, Six Months

The tragedy of three months ago dampened my initiative to write anything down. Even now, it's difficult to write about the event. Let me start from the beginning.

I was in the office early one morning working on papers for Washington. I had just sealed an envelope when a flash illuminated the room around me, similar to the flash that caused the blood in the seas. I ran to the window and looked down. Traffic stopped for a moment in the same fashion as the first time, but I gazed about the city and could not see anything peculiar from my office window. Turning on the radio, I listened to the news. They reported the flash was worldwide like before, but apparently no damage had occurred. Around noon, my wife called from home saying the school called about our son. Someone poisoned the water system at school and all the kids were being rushed to the hospital. I told her to go ahead to the hospital and call me from there.

An hour later, she called from the hospital. "Come down quick, hon. They say he might die soon."

At that moment, Washington called about reports I was late on. It took about half an hour to get off the phone. Rushing out of the office and down to the parking lot, I jumped into the car. On the way to the hospital, the radio announced the tragedy taking place. "Many think the substance to be wormwood, a perennial herb that originally was used in producing medicine and alcohol. The intake of contaminated water will cause death. I repeat, the intake of wormwood-contaminated water will result in death. At this time, it is estimated that one-third of the earth's water supply may have been contaminated. Do not, I repeat, do not drink any water until it can be proven to be uncontaminated."

Turning off the radio, I searched for a parking place anywhere near the hospital. Finally parking about half a mile away on a residential street, I jogged up to the emergency entrance where hundreds jammed the doorway. Trying to push my way through the crowd proved futile, so I ran around back and found another entrance to a hallway. As I began searching for my wife through the hospital, doctors and nurses dressed in white uniforms raced by me in both directions, paying no attention to my presence. I followed two of them carrying medical supplies into a hallway full of children and parents with hospital personnel attending to them. An unpleasant odor hit me as I looked up to see adults and children holding their stomachs and vomiting on the floor. Parents sobbed while their child lay dead in their arms and others just screamed, trying to gain the attention of a nurse or doctor.

Hearing a familiar cry from around a corner, I quickly darted through the crowd to spot my wife sitting on the floor holding our son. My daughter stood motionless, a look of fear across her face. Tears rolled down my wife's chin as she wept uncontrollably. Looking at the limp body upon her arms, I knew the fate. Without a word, I knelt down next to her and held her tight, while slowly stroking my hand through the knotted hair of our son. With his eyes shut for the last time, the King's name boldly glared from his forehead.

We decided upon a mini-funeral instead of a regular service. We both felt the sooner we moved on with our lives, the better. A lot of my employees stopped by to give their last respects, which I thought was very caring. Many had lost children and spouses from the contaminated water as well, but still found the time to stop by our son's funeral.

The King announced his great displeasure in the contamination of the water. Millions upon millions died around the world from approximately one-third of our entire water supply being contaminated by wormwood. Again he urged all people to hunt and kill any Jew or Christian. He said their

God is a wicked God who wants to destroy us all, but if we unite under him, we can rid ourselves of the plagues caused by their God.

The contamination of the water supply caused many economic problems. Water became so scarce in some areas of the country that the price of a gallon is over a dollar in some states. Many companies used the contaminated water for almost a day before finding out about it, resulting in millions of dollars in losses of soda, beer, juices, and food. Several smaller companies were forced to close due to the lack of fresh water. Others have taken the expense of shipping clean water all the way to their plants. In addition to our recession, we now have soaring food and water costs.

Last week, another strange event occurred. They announced on the news a great darkening taking place across our planet. According to the reports, one-third of the earth was darkened from the absence of sunlight, moonlight, or even starlight. Nothing but complete darkness. This darkness is occurring on the trailing edge of the earth's orbit around the sun. Thus, the first four hours of the morning and the last four hours of night have utter darkness. Once again, the phenomenon leaves scientists clueless as to its cause.

The next day following the broadcast, I woke up around six thirty. With my usual morning noncoherence, I failed to notice the darkness until walking outside to go to work. Stepping off our porch, I looked up at the street lights, which were still on. Puzzled, I glanced at my watch, wondering if I was up at the right time. It read seven thirty. Then I remembered the newscast of the night before.

At quarter to ten in the morning, most of the employees stopped working to see what would happen. I invited the managers into my room for donuts and coffee because of the view from my corner office on the top floor. At a few minutes past ten, the sun burst out, much like it does at the end of an eclipse. Within seconds, the sky exploded from darkness to full morning sunshine.

That night I decided to stay up to see if the darkness would set in again. At two a.m., the harvest moon and all stars disappeared as an eerie total blackness slowly spread over the night sky.

Four Years, Ten Months

The pain shoots within me like that of a scorpion's sting. It burns from my heart to my head. Breathing becomes a dreaded task, and closing my eyes focuses my mind on the pain rather than bringing relief. My head throbs far beyond the pain of a migraine headache. It feels like my brain could explode at any moment. I want it to. I want to die. Anything to rid myself of this torture. Oh, God, let me die. Please!

It began over one month ago. I had just finished work on our latest plan to ease the recession, and was enjoying the day off by working around the house with my partner. While we were working outside, a thick cloud mass rolled overhead, darkening the sky. My partner hollered, "Hon, look at the cloud bank."

"Good grief!" I answered. "Looks like smog rolling in fast motion."

"Hey, it could be rain!" she shouted with enthusiasm.

"I sure hope so!" I yelled as we ran inside.

We turned on the television to hear a special report on the cloud. The reporter spoke on how the entire earth had been covered with a thick smoke. No one knew why or where the smoke had come from. Some scientists ventured to say a delayed accumulation of smoke from the fires was causing an atmospheric cloud. As the reporter turned to interview a scientist, he let out an ear-piercing scream. He dropped the microphone on the ground and clutched his stomach and then the back of his head. He fell backward onto the ground while screaming. The screen flashed back to the news station, which immediately signed off and returned to an old western film.

My partner seemed as shocked as I was. She just stared at the television. I stood up and walked onto the front porch, watching the smoke clouds roll across the sky. A loud crash caused me to turn my head to see a car skid sideways in the street. Jumping off the porch, I ran down the street toward the accident. Loud screams came from inside the small vehicle, and I opened the door to find a woman doubled over, clutching herself in a similar fashion as the reporter. A police car siren whistled from behind and pulled up next to me. They quickly took over the situation and asked me about the accident. After explaining what I knew, I walked home and told my partner about the incident.

The evening news reported millions and millions of people suffering the same fate across the globe. The doctors had no clue as to what could be causing the sudden illnesses. Most thought it might be a strange new virus. Others claimed it was brought on by stress. (Which I think is ludicrous. How can so many people stress out at the same time, with no other reported incidents beforehand?) I think it is a new virus brought in by the smog cloud as indicated by many top scientists.

A scientist at UCLA explained the mysterious cloud as an intense smog. According to his theory (without getting too technical), the carbon monoxide and other smog chemicals had accumulated at the top of the earth's atmosphere for the last fifty years or so. With so much pollution being added from the fires of a few months ago, the atmosphere could no longer contain the smog. Thus, the cloud fell down to earth, becoming thicker by bonding with other chemicals in our air. According to him, the cloud could last quite some time. If we continue to abuse it with additional smog, it may never leave.

The next morning at work, over half the employees were out on sick leave. All reported the same symptoms of excruciating, internal pain. The rest of us waited anxiously for ten o'clock, to watch for the smog cloud after the darkening subsided. To our despair, the blackness departed to the smog cloud of yesterday, leaving the sun to shine at less than half strength.

Sometime before noon, one of my secretaries clutched her stomach and fell forward onto her desk. Blood gushed from her nose all over the desk. We called 911 and requested an ambulance. They told us only those with life-threatening situations could be transported because of the scarcity of emergency vehicles. I talked to the dispatcher and explained that my secretary had knocked herself out and we had not be able to stop the bleeding. The dispatcher finally agreed to send a vehicle.

As I hung up the phone, a sharp scream from down the hall pierced the air. I jumped out from behind my desk and ran toward the throng of people gathering in a room. Another employee was clutching her stomach and head while rolling on the floor. I made my way to her side and asked if I could help. She could only moan and gnash her teeth together. As I was ordering the crowd of employees to return to work, her boss pushed his way through and asked what happened. After I explained the situation, he thanked me and said he would take care of her.

The rest of the day continued in a similar fashion. Within two hours, over fifty more employees contracted the new virus. It was apparent by two o'clock that little work could be completed. The thought that maybe this virus was contagious became a fear. The authorities claimed it was from the smog cloud and not transmittable from person to person. Still, why take a chance? I talked with Washington about the crisis and they agreed. My division was dismissed at two fifteen, hoping that the fifty employees still left could come to work the next day.

I left by two thirty and picked up my partner from work on my way home. She spoke of similar events at her office. Her boss had keeled over right in front of her, and a man in the next cubicle fell against the wall when he contracted the virus. She had been asked to drive him home, but could not because she didn't have a car.

We continued our discussion about the virus and she expressed her fear of contracting it. I also expressed my feelings of concern and apprehensions. It was the first time in our lives that we really talked about any fears we had. I really felt the discussion brought us closer together and helped us to understand each other. I even asked God to spare her of this virus, willing to let it happen to me instead. Once at home she cooked us a splendid dinner with candlelight and wine. Unfortunately, our repose was short-lived.

While gathering the dishes from dinner, my partner screamed and dropped her glass onto the floor. Glancing up, I saw her head snap back and her body jerk backward toward the floor. I screamed her name at the top of my lungs and started toward her falling body. As I took a second step, a pain hit my heart like a snake biting through my chest and leaving its poisonous venom deep inside. The pain shot to my head like an electric shock. I remember failing toward the table, then blackness.

Several hours later, I woke up with my face buried in the carpet, still in agonizing pain. My eyes burned from within and I could barely breathe. Each quick gasp for air brought sharp pain to my neck and heart. Slowly moving my arms under my body, I pushed myself up, groaning out loud because of the throbbing.

My partner called for me in a weak voice. I turned my head just enough to spot her lying on the floor next to me. Her face and hands were smeared with dried blood and her dress was covered with cuts and blood stains. She closed her eyes and muttered something about hurting inside. Sliding toward her, I grabbed her hand with mine. While laying my head down next to hers, I told her I loved her.

We did not move the rest of the night or the next morning. The pain was just too great to do anything but lie motionless. We talked occasionally, but as little as possible for comfort's sake. The phone rang several times, but I could not motivate myself to even try answering.

Sometime after noon, the pain and throbbing disappeared.

It departed as quickly as it had come upon us. I looked up at my partner and proclaimed my relief. Recovering at the same moment, she rejoiced with me. Jumping up, we held each other tight. I noticed our daughter sitting on a chair, staring at us. We both ran over to her and hugged her. She didn't say a word as tears formed in her big, blue eyes.

The next hour was spent cleaning from the night before. I called work and explained what happened. One of my managers said everybody had come down with the virus, but those who received it first returned to work today, allowing us to continue operation.

We watched the news that evening, after a long nap to recuperate from the loss of sleep the night before. According to the reports, almost everyone on earth has been afflicted. Only a few select have yet to be struck down by the virus. My heart skipped when they reported a recurrence of the sickness amongst those who had been tormented before. They warned that the virus may strike more than once. However, the virus does not seem to leave any permanent damage, just torturous pain for a brief period of time. I wondered if we would have to go through this agony again. I only wondered for another day.

Two days after the virus first struck, I came down with it again, along with my partner. The entire population (except the Jews) also endured the same recurrence. It soon became apparent that this virus was here to stay. Every other day or so, we are afflicted from several hours to over a day. The same symptoms and pain come every time.

It has now been a month since I first received the virus. They have no cure and we have no hope of recovery. The virus hits with no warning or regularity and each time it hits, like now, I try to occupy my mind to relieve the torture. This helps to be able to function at least a little when the attacks occur. My partner, however, can't do anything but lie on the bed and cry. She often tries to reach a knife to put herself out of the misery, but her strength has failed every time.

The King cries against the God of the Jews and says we must terminate all Jews from the face of the earth to be free from their plagues. Oddly enough, neither the King nor the pope have contracted the virus, though every one of the ten presidents of the Federation have. He says that the God of the Jews cannot hurt him or the pope, because they are gods. He promises us we can all be gods soon, if we follow him and rid ourselves of the Jews.

I don't care how it happens, I just want to get rid of this pain!

Five Years

I actually cried today for the first time since I was thirteen. Men are not supposed to cry, but my heart is breaking. Instead of life becoming better, it continues to get worse. The God of the Jews hurts us for no reason at all. Why can't our King stop him?

Last night, my partner and daughter made a special dinner for my birthday. My little girl helped her mother in the kitchen preparing my big meal. The table was set with our imported china and silverware. The lights were turned off and only the candlelight shone in our dining room. They even bought a filet mignon for the occasion! I asked my partner where in the world she found a filet mignon. She just smiled and said, "I have my ways!"

They made me eat over half of the filet mignon by myself. I tried to give more to my partner, but she insisted upon eating only a few small bites. They even prepared two side dishes of corn and broccoli! To top it off, they brought out a cake with quite a few candles on it. The cake even had frosting! The whole meal was enjoyable and a nice change of pace from our normal eating habits. I felt really lucky to have the money for such a fancy meal and a family to be with.

After dinner, while my partner cleaned up from the meal, I played with my daughter. Chasing her around the house, we ended up in her bedroom. Quite a wrestling match broke out as my partner ran into the room to gang up on poor, defenseless me. I held my own until the pillow war ensued. They wouldn't let me have any pillows to defend myself! Laughing hysterically, we finally ended up falling into a heap on the bed.

I read my daughter a bedtime story and tucked her into

bed. Her straight blonde hair draped over the pillow as she turned her head. She whispered, "I love you, Daddy."

"I love you very much, too," I replied, kissing her cheek.

Her eyelids closed over her blue eyes as she yawned and exhaled a deep sigh. Rising from the side of her bed, I quietly walked to the doorway. The light from the hallway shone upon her bed. She looked so beautiful and peaceful. I slowly shut the door and released the knob, then joined my partner in the living room for a glass of wine and a romantic evening next to the fireplace.

This morning, while drying myself from a shower, my partner let out an ear-splitting scream. Quickly wrapping the towel around my body, I ran into the hallway, hearing her sobs come from our daughter's room. I opened the door and saw my wife kneeling on the floor, sprawled across the bed. Jolting to her side, I touched my daughter's face. The cold from her body sent chills through my arm and back. "No!" I screamed, "not again!"

I knelt down next to my partner and put my arm around her. Tears formed in my eyes and began to roll down my cheeks. Taking a deep breath, I exhaled in gasps. I began to sniffle and feel my head swell and pound. My partner slid from the bed and into my arms, and we wept for several minutes, not knowing what to do or say. I finally wiped my eyes dry enough to stand up and walk to the phone, calling for the funeral parlor to pick her up. They said they would pick her up as soon as they could, but many people died last night all over town, and we were down the list a ways.

Around eight thirty work called to inform me of over twenty employees who died last night. I told my partner of the emergency situation at work and that I would return home as soon as possible. She held me for a long moment and kissed my cheek without saying a word. I rushed to work in hopes of getting the mess straightened out and returning home early. However, the situation at work was much worse than expected. Over one hundred of our employees in my division died the night before, postponing my return home until late in the evening. We watched the news at ten report of over one billion people dying with no explanation of how or why. It reminded me of the plague a few years back, and this time it took my precious treasure.

Five Years, Four Months

The sores cover my fingertips, as well as the rest of my body. It hurts to press each key on this computer. Each touch I make sends a burning sensation through my body. The slightest movement in my chair sends pain up my spine. The stench from these sores smells like rotten flesh, and it nauseates me every time I get a whiff from my hands or someone standing next to me. I sleep with only a light sheet over my body, but even that hurts at the slightest movement. The few meals we eat have become a task rather than a pleasure. Holding a fork or spoon can be done only by finding spots on my hands without the sores, and trying to cut anything with a knife is even worse. The food itself tastes terrible due to the smell rising from my hands when I bring a bite to my mouth. Even wearing clothes hurts from the fabric touching the sores. It is not uncommon to see people walking naked on the streets, looking like ghosts from the powder covering their grotesque sores.

This torture began about three weeks ago. I remember sitting at my desk in the afternoon when my chest and back started to itch. By the time the office closed, I was scratching all over my body with no relief from the irritation. Everyone in my division developed the same symptoms. Once home, I took off my clothes and noticed numerous red spots all over my body. That night in bed, I slept only in sporadic spurts due to the itching. Blood oozed from the now-open wounds where I scratched repeatedly. My partner suffered with the same rash and we both wanted a shower, but had to wait until morning. Because of the shortage, water was shut off every night at eight, not available again until six in the morning.

After the sleepless night, we both hopped into a relieving cool shower. For the first time since the afternoon before, I did not itch. The water rolling down from my head soothed my skin. The blood from the sores mixed with the water and washed into the drain. I stepped out of the shower and dried myself. The sores hurt again as I patted myself with the towel. I put my clothes on and could feel them rub against my sores. Then, along with the pain, my body started itching again. I knew I was in for a miserable day.

That one miserable day has turned into three wretched weeks. The sores grew worse throughout that first day and opened into smelling wounds. The itching became intolerable and the pain increased substantially. By the next day, taking a shower hurt more than wearing clothes. Even though it relieved the itching, the water ran over the open sores, causing a sting like that of alcohol over an open wound. Many people refuse to take showers because of the pain, causing the smell to intensify even more. After these three weeks, I refuse to go to any place with even a small crowd. The stench nauseates me, and I invoked a rule at work that if anyone did not shower daily, that person would be fired.

To relieve the itching and cover the smell, doctors recommend covering your body with talcum powder. To further allow for workable conditions, I passed another rule allowing employees to wear whatever is comfortable, as long as everything is covered. Many of the women are now wearing halter tops and men's shorts. Most of the men wear t-shirts or tank tops with baggy shorts. No one wears anything but sandals or thongs on their feet, because shoes and socks are just too painful to make anyone wear, including myself!

The King blames the God of the Jews and two preachers in Jerusalem for all the problems. The two preachers walk through Jerusalem in sackcloth and ashes. No one knows where they came from or who they are, but they arrived sometime before the King took power in Israel. They preach to everyone to repent from sin and prepare for the Kingdom of Jesus Christ. The King sent troops out to kill them, but a stream of fire came from their mouths and destroyed their pursuants!

Several others have tried to kill them, but all have met the same fate. They have brought many plagues into Jerusalem, and the King blames them for the recent ones as well. It's a well-known fact that the great drought began almost the same time they appeared in Jerusalem. No one took notice at that time, but since there has been no rain in two years, it's obvious they are to blame.

I wonder, though, why our King can't destroy these two. One would think that he would have the power to be able to do it, yet he continues to allow them to preach through his own city. He claims they are from the God of the Jews and soon he will be able to overcome them. I am also sick of the terrible things happening to us. This God of the Jews seems to be very wicked. Why does he send these plagues on us? Why does he not let us live in peace under our King?

Five Years, Eleven Months

One glass of water is all I want. Just one cool, refreshing, clean glass of water. I am sick of this blood. It nauseates me to even think about it. The smell is enough to gag anyone, much less having to actually drink it. Oh, God, why are you doing this to us? How can we survive without water? People can't survive by drinking blood, can they?

I made it until yesterday without actually having to drink any blood. My supply of bottled drinks expired five days ago. I managed without anything to drink at all until yesterday, when the craving for liquid was just too strong for my throat to handle. The price for any canned drink or bottled water is over three hundred dollars! I just couldn't afford to buy any. With the blood running out of our faucets, I finally decided to quench my thirst with a small glass of blood. Everyone else I know has already been drinking blood for quite some time because they did not have the money to buy water or drinks that were bottled before the catastrophe over two months ago.

Turning on the faucet, I watched the red liquid pour into the sink and down the drain. I shivered thinking about actually having to drink it. I tried to swallow, but I had no spit to even wet my tongue. My glass filled under the stream of blood. Turning the faucet off, I looked at the glass. The smell filled my nostrils and nauseated my stomach. Putting the glass down, I walked out of the kitchen, thinking that I was incapable of actually drinking blood. About an hour later I walked back into the kitchen and grabbed the glass. I shut my eyes and held my nose while quickly gulping two swallows. My body shivered and my stomach rejected the new liquid back into the sink. After a few moments, my eyes quit watering and the convulsions passed. My tongue swished around inside my mouth, feeling actual liquid for the first time in days. The taste of the blood disgusted me, but the sensation of having liquid on my tongue and in my throat surpassed the grotesque taste. Three glasses later, my stomach held down the blood as I became accustomed to its taste and texture.

About five months ago, just after our sores finally disappeared, the seas and oceans turned into blood. Every known creature in the sea died and floated to the top. The entire shipping industry came to a standstill. Dead creatures covered the top of the waters (or blood, as it were), making travel an impossibility for any ship or boat. The offensive odor drives people away from the beaches and coastal areas. People in New York City, Los Angeles, and just about every metropolitan area along the shores wear masks in order to diminish the stench. The famed beaches of the Riviera, Florida, Hawaii, and others which once were the most sought after vacation spots, have lost their appeal and their tourist trade. Every resort located on a salt water body closed down, while many tourist cities became ghost towns almost overnight. The once-beautiful white beaches turned into blood dried sand with dead marine animals several feet deep.

Then two months ago, every fresh water supply turned to blood. Every lake, river, and spring pumped blood rather than clean water. Fresh water was not to be found anymore, except for the already bottled water and drinks made before the disaster. It was then that my partner and I ran out and bought as much bottled and canned drinks as we could. The prices were so high though, we bought only enough to ration out for two months.

Personal hygiene has also been greatly affected. I really miss being able to take a shower or bath. What I wouldn't give to be able to step into a steaming hot bath of water, or a cold one for that matter. The feeling of actually being clean from all of this dirt, sweat, and grime would be so exhilarating. To think, I used to take a daily shower or bath for granted!

To combat the smell, we spray deodorant and perfumes all over our bodies, but it doesn't cover the feeling of being dirty all the time. Even worse, many people cannot afford to buy deodorant at all, which means standing in a crowd without a mask may bring tears to one's eyes.

We can't wash clothes, sheets, or dishes. What little water remained was used strictly for drinking. My partner takes out the sheets and clothes every other day or so, hangs them up on a line, and beats them with a broom. Then she sprays disinfectant on them. We also haven't washed the dishes since the day of the catastrophe. A manufacturer did develop a powder disinfectant designed specifically for putting on dishes when scraping the plates. Though it cost a lot, my wife bought some and we have found it quite sanitary compared to anything else we can do.

Time saves me from talking about the sewage, food, and many other problems caused by the latest in a series of disasters. I only hope this is the last one and we can move into our new age. My partner can barely handle it anymore. She has thrown two fits of rage in the last month. Even I don't know how long I'll last!

Six Years, Four Months

Once again I write to take my mind off the pain and suffering. The heat is unbearable. We have yet to have a day or night of temperatures under one hundred degrees in almost five months. I gnaw my tongue to the point of bleeding because of the pain. We live in utter darkness continually. We have not seen the light of the sun or moon in almost two months. The God of the Jews is sending these terrible problems upon us. I hate Him. Why doesn't He understand that we don't want Him to rule over us. We want our King. I wish he would go away and leave us in peace.

About five months ago, just after I wrote last, the temperatures skyrocketed into the hundreds. I remember sitting at my desk about four in the afternoon and hearing on the radio that the temperature had been rising since three o'clock instead of dropping like it normally does. From two p.m. until just after three, the temperature hung at eighty degrees. Then it rose to ninety-seven degrees at four o'clock. Finishing work, I continued to listen to the news reports on why the temperature was rising so sharply over the entire globe at the same time. Even though most people blamed the God of the Jews, a few fanatics still tried to explain it as the greenhouse effect. I laughed thinking about the fools who still try to explain these disasters as natural phenomena.

Around five thirty, I walked out of the office and down to the front doors. I reached out to pull the glass doors open, but could open it only about two inches on my first try. I tugged at it again, but for some reason the door was being suctioned from outside. Bracing my left foot against the side, I yanked with both my hands. The door slowly gave way and I could feel the air rush past me from inside. Bracing my right foot against the door, I grabbed my briefcase. As I lifted up my foot, the door shoved me out and cracked my other heel. I yelped and grabbed my foot while dancing on the other one. Then the heat buffeted my face like a blast furnace. The temperature was a scorching one hundred and twenty degrees! I took half of a deep breath and began coughing from the burning sensation in my lungs. Sweat formed on my head and under my arms. Digging into my pocket, I pulled out my handkerchief to wipe my forehead. Walking to my car, I anticipated turning on the air conditioning, but I noticed several cars sitting on the side of the street with steam pouring out of the engines. The few cars still driving around all had their windows down. It became apparent that I would not be able to drive with the air conditioner on.

On my trip home, I thought about having a cool, tall glass of water. I reminisced about going home, popping open the refrigerator, grabbing one of the many drinks inside, and guzzling an entire can in a few short seconds. If I was sweaty, I could take a long, refreshing shower and feel cleansed. How I long for those days again. I cringed thinking about having to drink blood to quench this growing thirst. I would not even be able to take a shower! The hot breeze flowing through the opened windows could not hide the smell coming from my sweaty body. It had been months since my last shower. No amount of deodorant or cologne could hide this stench. What I would give for just one clean shower of five minutes!

That night, the temperatures dropped to about one hundred five degrees after sunset. We kept the air conditioning set at ninety-five degrees and set up fans over our bed. The most difficult part in trying to sleep wasn't the heat but the smell from both of our bodies and the sheets. I now stuff cotton up my nose at night to avoid the unpleasant aroma. I also wondered if our electric bill would send me to the poor house.

The next day, the air conditioning at our work shut down when the temperatures reached one hundred thirty degrees at noon. I immediately dismissed all the employees to go home. Many of them, including myself, went down into the basement where the temperature hovered at only one hundred degrees. We set up tables and chairs and worked together on all the projects Washington wanted us to finish. We actually had fun laughing at each other and teasing about who smelled worse. They voted me as the worst smelling.

The temperatures for the day reached one hundred thirty-eight degrees! Many people died from heat exhaustion and heart attacks. Any food left in the heat rotted after just a few minutes. Plastic molding in cars melted. Any street with tar mixture became too sticky to even cross with a car. Anyone staying in the sun for over ten minutes developed second degree burns on their exposed skin. Just standing outside caused sweat to literally drip from one's body. The only way to avoid dehydration is to drink blood … and lots of it!

One form of relief is to freeze the blood and put it into packets. Then rub them over one's body or put them in the bathtub and lie in it. This way, one can avoid the unpleasantness of dried blood smeared over their bodies and still keep their temperatures down. As the blood melts, one can either refreeze it immediately or drink it.

After a week of one hundred forty degree temperatures, it became apparent that working during daylight would be almost useless. People could not concentrate on their work, plus many people suffered from heat exhaustion and dehydration. In response, the government passed an emergency law allowing working hours to be only from sunset to sunrise. During the day, everyone was encouraged to stay inside and find some way to beat the heat.

I found working at night to be quite a hassle. Trying to sleep during the day is almost an impossibility. About every hour I wake up and change the blood bags on my body. I think the longest I've slept in any given period without waking up is two hours. My employees can't concentrate on their work because of the one hundred ten degree temperature even down in the basement. Many of them spend half the time cursing God, spraying deodorant, waving a fan in their face, or complaining about the smell.

The oddness of the whole ordeal is the switch in hours. I used to get up at seven in the morning and go to work. Now I get up at seven in the evening instead! I eat breakfast at the same time I used to eat supper. Businesses are open only during the evening hours. Even television has been affected. Prime time is between the hours of four and seven in the morning when people are arriving home from work and before they try to get some sleep. During daylight hours, not one single person can be found outside in the sun. All sit in their homes, trying to escape the heat in one way or another.

For five months now, we dread daytime and the extreme temperatures it brings. We lie in bed or on a couch and plug a fan in over us to stay as cool as possible. 'The only movement I ever make during the day is to go to the freezer and replenish my supply of frozen bags of blood. My heart goes out to those in other parts of the world without fans to keep cool or refrigerators to freeze blood. Many die in other countries from heat exhaustion. I am thankful we still have such luxuries as electric fans and refrigerators. Luckily, I can still afford the gas to drive to work in the evening. Almost everyone else uses the bus or has moved closer to work. I don't know if I could deal with the smell or the heat in a bus. My employees tell me horror stories of drinking enough blood not to get dehydrated and still watching someone die from heat exhaustion almost every night on the trip to or from work.

The city banned the use of air conditioners due to the power shortage. Only hospitals are allowed to use them in some of their rooms. To cool the entire hospital uses too much power, so certain areas are designated for surgery and intensive care. Even then, they can keep the temperature only a little below one hundred! If the government did allow us to use air conditioners, it would not matter because the air conditioners shut down or are useless once the temperature rises above one hundred thirty. They also cost more than one week's salary to run for just one day!

About two months ago, the great darkening that covered one third of the earth expanded to cover the whole world. I was lying in my bed late one afternoon when the sunlight just disappeared. After reaching over to turn on the light, I ran to the window, hoping to see rain clouds. To my disappointment, neither the clouds nor the sun could be seen. Everything was pitch black up in the sky. I walked out my front door to see what had happened and noticed my other neighbors were looking around, too. The street lights came on to illuminate the surrounding areas, but the darkness seemed thicker than normal. The street lights did not shine like they usually did. I could tell the darkness was evil.

I started to curse God and tell him what I thought about the evil he was sending us, but the heat quickly drained my energy and evaporated my sweat. Moving back into the kitchen, I drank two big glasses of blood. I grabbed several bags of frozen blood and slowly walked back to my bed. My partner lay there moaning in her sleep. I looked at the sores on her shoulders and face. They were acting up again. While sitting on the edge of my bed, it dawned on me that the temperature was not dropping. Why not? With the sun being blocked out, the temperature should at least drop to one hundred and twenty or so, like it does at night!

I began gasping for fresh air and lay down on my back. twitching from the pain of my sores touching the mattress. Wiping the sweat from my brow with my arm. I placed one of the bags of blood on my head. I placed the other two on my chest and stomach. The thought of getting up in a couple of hours to go to work depressed me. I hated to put on gloves so I could touch the car and steering wheel. I hated the drive to work and the heat blasting through the rolled-down windows. I hated the stench from the other workers and having to look at the ugly sores all over their faces. I hated lying in bed and not being able to move because of the pain from my sores. I hated drinking blood. I hated the sweat and smell from the high temperatures. I hated not having a big steak or a decent meal. I hated not being able to exercise or take a shower. I hated the two witnesses who brought plagues and caused the rain to cease. I hated not having my children to play with. I hated not having a normal relationship with my partner anymore. I hated the filth that covers my body because I can't take a shower or clean myself. I hated gnawing my tongue and bleeding in my mouth because of all the pain. I hated living. I despised the thought of God. I abhorred every plague and misery he sent. I hated God.

It's been two months since then, and we still have not seen the sun, stars, or moon. We live in darkness and misery. Sores still cover my body and my tongue hurts and bleeds from chewing it raw. I live a miserable and useless life. My only dream is to rid earth of the God of the Jews. Our King claims we can beat him if we unite. He promises us victory if we can just make it a little longer.

I hate God. He has ruined our lives. Soon we will have victory over him. We have to. We just have to. The God of the Jews must die!

Six Years, Nine Months

I despise the day I was born. I spit at the mirror and curse the God of the Jews who brings us this misery. The memories plunge through my mind: blue skies, clean water, green grass, mouth-watering steak, chocolate, cool evenings, playing basketball with the guys, watching football on the television, vacations at the beach, long drives in the country, walking in the parks, a refreshing shower, a snow-covered field, cuddling with my wife next to the fireplace, watching my kids play, family dinners, eating out for lunch, laughing, and smiling. All seem an eternity away. Our only hope lies with victory over the God of the Jews. Our King will prevail … he must!

Four months ago our King announced that all the armies of the world should gather in Israel to fight the God of the Jews and his slaves. Promising victory if we would unite under him, the King urged every able-bodied man and woman to join their country in fighting the God of the Jews. Our King shall reign supreme if we can prove to God that we no longer want him to rule over us.

The anticipation of finally being released from God's miserable tyranny enticed hundreds of millions to sign up and leave for the country of Israel. The United States began airlifting troops within two weeks of the King's announcement. We also sent planes to help the Central and South Americans to reach Israel. Over thirty million from the Americas have been sent, with more leaving every day.

Two weeks after the King's announcement, the great River Euphrates dried up. No one knows why this odd phenomenon would occur, but it sure helps the coming troops traveling from the East. Immediately afterward, China, India, and Japan announced their support for the King and arranged for troop dispersal. Because fuel is scarce, most of the hundreds of millions of troops from the East are walking instead of driving or flying. Because of the heat, they camp during the day and march at night. Reports still show everyone in high spirits as the troops gather to fight for our own planet and home.

Until two days ago, I spent the last three months working and trying to survive like everyone else. It was then, while walking to the freezer to replenish my frozen blood, that I heard a low rumbling noise from outside. The events of the last few years prevented me from running to the window in hopes of the much desired rain. Instead, I slowly peered out the window and up into the sky, fearing what the next disaster might be. The ominous, black clouds filled the already dark sky like a fast-motion video picture. I screamed to my partner back in the

bedroom, "Hon, do you see the clouds?"

"Yes, I'm watching them right now."

I ran back to the bedroom as the sweat poured down my body and dripped onto the floor.

"Do you think it's going to finally rain?" my wife asked.

"I would sure like to think so, but my senses tell me otherwise."

We watched the skies fill with angry clouds. Each moment heightened my already intense anxiety. Logic prevented a feeling of relief, but deep down flickered a slight bit of hope. Might it be possible that these were rain clouds to end the three-year drought? Maybe just maybe, the new age was finally arriving. Still, I could feel my stomach turning inside out from fear rather than hope.

"Look at all the lightning flash!" my partner exclaimed. "It has to be rain coming."

"Either that or God is flaunting more of his power," I retorted.

My wife began, "I think …" but she stopped. Her eyes

fastened to an object next to the window.

Following her eyes, I now noticed the drapes wiggling back and forth. I heard glasses and porcelain clinking around our room. My heart sank and I felt a lump well up in my throat. I knew immediately what it was. "Earthquake. Get outside!" I screamed.

I grabbed my partner's arm and yanked her toward the bedroom door. We started to run, but slowed to a wobbling walk as the quake grew in magnitude. Small chunks of plaster fell from the ceiling all around us, and I could hear lamps and plates crashing to the floor behind us. I cringed as a piece of plaster bounced off the top of my head. My wife began screaming, and tugging at my hand. "We must get outside; it's the only safe spot!" I yelled over the growing rumbling noise of the quake.

I half pushed my wife through the door to get her outside. One of the posts holding the porch roof cracked loudly in front of us. Immediately, we both jumped and landed on the cement, bouncing into the dirt face first. The roof collapsed behind us with a deafening crunch, followed by the shattering of the front windows. I tried to look to my partner to see if she was hurt, but the shaking was so violent all I could do was grasp the ground and close my eyes.

As I lay on the ground, I could hear our house creak and finally fall. The end had finally come. What better way to die than in a huge earthquake? I waited for the ground to open up and swallow me. Why was it taking so long? I could feel my neck and back pop with each jerk back and forth. Let's just get it over with, I thought. My head hit the ground and dirt shot into my mouth and nose. The darkness closed in and the noise faded away.

I woke up with the earth lying beneath me in a relieved stillness. I cleaned the dirt out of my mouth and nose by spitting and puffing air. Slowly lifting my head, I turned to see my partner. Her outstretched arms clung tightly to the earth. Her fingers were partially buried into the dirt from grasping the once-shaking ground. Her long, light brown hair straggled over her pale cheeks. I crawled toward her and muttered, "Hon, are you okay?"

She opened her eyes and cracked a grin. "We made it, didn't we?"

"We sure did."

She released her grip and pushed herself up to meet me. As we moved our lips to kiss, several objects bounced off my back and head. I lifted my face into the sky, only to feel the hail pelt my cheeks and brow. "Oh, no. Quick, we've got to find shelter," I said, dropping my voice in disappointment.

I grabbed my partner's hand as we stood up. The house lay in ruins before us. The crushed boards and bricks stood in a pile no taller than five feet. I gazed about the neighborhood, looking for shelter from the increasing hailstorm. Every house, building, and tree was thrown down to the ground as far as I could see. Our only hope was to find an opening under the pile of scraps left from the house and try to hide.

The hail increased to golf ball size as we began diligently searching for a place of refuge. Each ice ball caused sharp pain as it landed on my shoulders, back and head. I found a spot under a portion of the broken porch big enough for one person to crawl under. I pushed my wife toward it and said, "Quick, get in."

"No, no, you take it," she opposed.

"Ouch! "I yelled as a baseball-size hailstone found its mark upon my head, causing a bright flash and an immediate headache. "Hurry up and get in, so I can find a spot!"

She dropped down to her hands and knees and crawled into the small opening. I quickly moved back around the remains of the house while holding a broken piece of wood over my head. I began cursing at God as the hail grew to softball size, splintering the wood and crushing my fingers. I finally found an opening in the back under the former stairwell, just big enough to squeeze in on my stomach. I threw the board to the side and scurried head first into the dark cave.

I could feel the hail pound my calves and feet as I pushed the dirt and pieces of wood aside to fit into the hole. I bent sideways and curled my legs up underneath to fit all the way into the shelter. The pounding of the hail grew louder and stronger. It sounded like bowling bails or even bigger size ones hitting the pile of rubble above me. I took a deep breath and felt the beam above my back. I exhaled and drew in another breath. This time the beam withheld my complete inhale of air. "Oh no," I thought out loud, "I'm going to die by being crushed."

The sweat stung my eyes as I heard the hail crushing the wood above me. The beam lowered more and pushed the air out of my lungs. I frantically moved my arms and body to draw in another breath. I gulped a quick breath and screamed at the top of my lungs, "No! I hate you God!"

After all I'd been through, God was going to crush me under my own house. Curses toward the God of the Jews filled my mind. Trapped like a rat without a fight. What a coward! God won't even face me. I moved the last inch I could move and drew in what I thought was my last breath. Then it stopped. An eerie silence surrounded me.

I hesitated for just a moment, then squirmed my way backward out of the hole. My feet barely pushed the beach ball-sized hail to the side as I wiggled back and forth. I broke free and lifted myself to my knees. The deep breaths of fresh air relaxed my entire body. I had survived again!

I brushed my hands off and grabbed one of the melting hail stones. I put it in my mouth and tasted fresh water for the first time in years. The coldness exploded on my tongue and cheeks. It brought memories of drinking water from a glass and eating the ice after the liquid was gone. Within seconds it melted and I grabbed for another piece. I popped another piece into my mouth and rubbed another one all over my body. The refreshing coldness sent chills up my spine. The sensation surpassed anything I had felt in years. It lasted for only a moment. Before I could even eat another ice bail, they melted in my hand and through my fingers. As quickly as the hail landed, it disappeared into the soil.

I glanced back to the front of the house to see if my partner had tasted of the refreshment as well. The darkness hindered any effort of seeing her, so I started to walk around the house while scrutinizing the remains. Upon reaching the place where my wife hid, I searched for the opening. It was nowhere to be found! I looked about the area to make sure this was the same place. My heart began racing as I frantically removed pieces of wood from the pile. "Babe, do you hear me? Please answer!" I cried.

Each piece of wood felt cold and rough. Splinters and broken glass dug deep into my hand, drawing droplets of blood. Nothing slowed my frantic removal of debris. She must be here somewhere. I continued to call her name with each broken board I removed.

The darkness could not hide the cold, clammy piece of flesh I felt under one of the boards. My hand slid down the muscle, through the thickening blood, to the familiar shoe. In a frenzy, I threw the boards over my back to uncover the body below. I gently slid my arms under her midsection and lifted her out of the hole. Her body felt heavier than anything I had ever lifted before.

Slowly and tenderly, I set her down on the ground as teardrops formed in my eyes. I sat down beside her and pulled her arms around me like she had done for over fifteen years. Tears flowed down my cheeks and dripped to the ground. I flared my nostrils and took in a deep breath, trying to hold back the crying. I ran my fingers through the tangled hair and pushed it off her face. This time her eyes did not open to look at me. Instead, her eyelids covered the once responsive keys to my heart. I stroked her cheeks and neck with the back of my hand. I pressed her head against my chest and sobbed uncontrollably.

I looked up into the dark sky and shoved my clenched fist into the empty air. "I hate you, God! I will make you pay for this! You will pay for this!"

Six Years, Ten Months

I took a long walk through our neighborhood tonight, reminiscing on the good old days.

The corner mini-market was the mainstream of the neighborhood with its central location and convenience. I think everybody stopped there once a week from our neighborhood to get gas or pick up some milk. The young woman behind the counter always smiled whenever a customer walked in. My flashlight shone upon the broken awning over the once-busy gas pumps. Though the business closed several years ago after the gas shortage and famine, the fallen building brought the realization that the pumps would never serve another customer again.

Shining my light around, I continued walking along the streets I had grown so accustomed to over the years. Most of the homes were abandoned heaps of wood. Others were partially broken houses with families or groups of people making the best of what was left. Every occupied house had a fire in the front, which gave light and protection from the wild animals. I could look down the street and see a fire blazing about every tenth house or so. I looked for kids to be playing or doing something while the temperature was down below one hundred ten degrees, but the only people outside sat on crates or makeshift chairs about twenty feet from the fires.

After several blocks, I saw a young boy digging in the dirt in front of his house where the grass once flourished and bushes grew. He scraped the ground with a broken piece of wood, seemingly searching for some sort of treasure. His mom or guardian yelled from inside the house about the dust being raised and he immediately stopped. He dropped his head and tossed the board to the side. In his boredom, he began gazing about the empty dirt lawn in hopes of finding something to occupy his mind. My flashlight caught his attention for a moment, but he turned away as I passed by without stopping or talking.

I continued my stroll through the business section by the freeway. The streets remained empty save for an occasional pack of three or four young kids walking around and wreaking havoc upon the fallen buildings. How different it was just a few years ago when these same streets bustled with activity. My wife used to shop along here in her sunglasses and white hat. She would bring the kids and beg me to go along. Only when I didn't have a good excuse would I force myself to endure the crowds and hassle. As much as I hated shopping before, I'd give anything to be able to do it just one more time with her.

I sat down on the dusty curb, needing to rest a moment and wipe the sweat off my face. While sitting there, I heard an engine noise from around the corner. A pickup truck turned onto my street. The headlights blinded me momentarily, so I rubbed them with my fists. The truck stopped in front of me and four men armed with machine guns hopped out of the back and hovered over me.

"Can I see your identification?" one asked.

I held up the back of my hand with the King's name and reached into my pocket with the other. I slid my wallet out and held up my government employee identification card. He carefully scrutinized the plastic card.

"He's okay," the man said, turning to his fellow gunman. "How come you haven't gone to Israel?" he asked, turning back to me.

"I'm leaving tomorrow night," I replied.

"How come you haven't left until now? You only have a few weeks before the Great Victory," he questioned.

"Because of my job in the government. They wanted me to remain here. But since the earthquake, they decided to close up most of the government branches, including mine. They chose me to be a government supervisor and observer at the Great Victory."

"Cool! Does that mean you just watch the action'?"

"Yep, that's right. I'm being sent to the city of Bethshan, and then Megiddo. I check on all the United States troops and report their activities back to Washington. I will then be allowed to observe the Great Victory from one of the mountains overlooking the Plain of Esdraelon."

"Wow. I envy you. I wish I was going."

The other officers expressed their admiration and wished me the best. One of them even offered me some cool blood to quench my thirst. I gladly accepted. The last time I had anything cold were the hailstones of a month and a half ago. The truck pulled away and slowly bounced down the street in search of other passersby.

My mind raced with excitement. In just twenty hours I would be leaving for Jerusalem. I would then be picked up, along with other national officials, and taken to Bethshan for meetings with top officials from the King's army. They would brief us on the entire world army movement and battle plans. We would then be transported to Megiddo for other meetings and possibly get to meet the King. Finally, we would travel with a platoon through the Plain of Esdraelon. I would be allowed to pick any spot in the valley or on a hill to observe the Great Victory. The celebration might go on for weeks! What an opportunity! Coming back to reality, I stood up from the curb and continued my journey through the neighborhood.

The school my son had attended stood alone on the city block. The solid stone structure somehow withstood the earthquake, though all the windows were broken out. My son had played on the grassy playground with his laughing classmates. He had learned about the world and its history. He had dreamed of the future and how he would make his mark in it. Instead of hope, the abandoned building reeked of despair. As I continued my trek homeward, the memories of my family clouded over the excitement of the trip.

I did not want to travel to Israel. I wanted to go back home to my wife and kids. I wanted my house with the recliner and television waiting for me. I wanted a tail, cool glass of milk and a juicy steak to fill my stomach. I wanted to wake up to find this was all a bad dream. A sweat drop caught the edge of my eye, bringing me back to reality. There was nothing left for me here. Only memories.

I imagined what it would be like to come back after the Great Victory. The skies shining bright and the grass growing again. If a job in Washington didn't work out, I might start up a business here. I have enough connections to come up with the money. It would be great to be a part of the reconstruction of our town. Everyone pulling together to build new homes and town buildings. The fresh, new beginning we've dreamed about!

The fire in front of the collapsed house had dwindled to a red glow. I grabbed some more wood and threw it on. The yellow flames slowly danced about the broken boards. For a moment, my wife sat next to me on the couch and hugged my, neck. Her eyes glistened from the fire as we sipped wine together.

I could feel the temperature rising as daytime quickly approached. I shone my light around the mattress, looking for bugs and other animals which might have decided to settle in my bed. The mattress and pillow needed heavy beating to rid them of dirt and unwanted creatures. I shook out the sheet and covered myself from the stomach down. This would be my last time to sleep here. Tomorrow at the same time, I would be in Israel. My eyes slowly closed and the crackling fire lulled me to sleep.

Six Years, Ten Months, Two Weeks

Day One

The plane trip to Jerusalem was terrible. We were packed in like the proverbial sardines. People sat in the aisles and in the cargo compartment. With the oil shortage, every jet must be filled to capacity with those going to the Great Victory. The smell inside the cabin was worse than my high school locker room after a football game. No matter how much deodorant or perfume people put on, it can't cover the stench of three and a half years with no showers.

After the landing, an official from the King's army waited for me at the bottom of the stairs coming off the plane. He introduced himself and welcomed me to Israel. His gray hair and small body seemed amazingly clean. The soap scent from his hand lingered in my nose for a moment. Before I could question him, he asked if I would enjoy a glass of ice water to drink and a bucket of water to clean with. My eyelids rose as I nodded quick approval.

The official whisked me away from the airport in a black limousine to a nearby hotel. He arranged for a full meal with a small steak, vegetables, and the water he promised. After the dinner, I washed with a cloth and soapy water. Words cannot describe the contentment of a full stomach and a clean body. I will sleep well today!

Day Two

A different official woke me up about nine p.m. It felt wonderful to sleep in after the royal treatment of the night before. For the first time in months, I woke up fresh and satisfied.

I went to meetings all day long in the hotel with other

country government representatives. About one hundred representatives from as many countries sat in the conference. Several of the King's army officials spoke to us about our schedule and plans. We must follow strict guidelines and rules in our special participation in the Great Victory.

Day Three

They woke us up at six p.m. sharp. Two buses transported the group to Hadera on the outskirts of the Plain of Esdraelon. Another hotel and meeting room awaited our arrival and we spent about two hours in meetings after another steak dinner! I don't know where they managed to get such great food, but I haven't been treated so well since a trip to Washington over three years ago!

Day Four

Today the group traveled to Haifa, on the northern edge of the Plain of Esdraelon. After another outstanding dinner, the group was told to get some rest for tomorrow. A big day was in store with some surprises. The crowd buzzed with excitement over the possibility of meeting the King!

I have developed a friendship with an official from Canada. He lost his wife in the first plague of death almost five years ago. He lost one of his children in the fires and his other two during the contamination of the water. Since then, he has worked for the Canadian government in the same capacity as myself. We spend most of our free time playing gin and talking about our plans after the Great Victory.

Day Five

What an incredible day!

We awoke at six for fresh water to wash with and a special breakfast treat. They provided actual donuts and fruit juices for everyone! We knew something big was up.

The group was rushed to a government building and escorted into a banquet hail. After being seated, our guide explained how lucky we were to have arrived the last day of the King's summit meeting in Haifa. All the military leaders gathered here the last few days for meetings on the Great Victory. He proudly announced the willingness of several leaders to brief us on their actions before leaving for the front. After several more flattering statements, he introduced the commander-in-chief of the world army! The crowd roared with approval as the commander briefed us on the maneuvers of the different forces involved in the Great Victory. He brought one of his own military maps that was passed around the room. He lectured for over an hour before having to leave to return to the front lines. We gave him a standing ovation for over five minutes.

After finally settling the crowd down, our guide asked for complete silence. "Please stand!" he commanded.

The group rose to their feet with anticipation. World army troops filed into the room, armed heavily with machine guns and explosives. They surrounded the podium and stage where our guide stood. He continued, with cracking in his voice, "It is my honor and pleasure to introduce to you . . . the King! Please bow to our Lord."

I immediately dropped to one knee and lowered my head. Whispers of "Praise the King," and "Great is our Lord," could be heard around the room.

"Please, be seated," stated a deep, but unusually calming voice.

I sat down and looked up at the magnificent King. My eyes squinted from the brightness of his white uniform and the glow around him. His broad-shouldered body filled the uniform with incredulous perfection. His totally blond hair and slightly tanned skin enhanced the brightness of his white teeth. Every part of his body was put together in the most pleasing way. I had never seen such beauty in a man before. Television cameras could not do him justice.

His deep, soft voice soothed my innermost being. Every fear and doubt melted with each word spoken from his lips.

Yet, his voice echoed with authority … a firm confidence of power and complete supremacy. I felt safe and secure being in the same room with him, though my body shook with the awe of his presence.

"Ladies and gentlemen, I want to welcome you to the Great Victory. We are pleased to have a representative from each country to write about the splendor of the world army and the glorious victory for each of their respective nations. I hope you have been treated well and have found your living quarters most satisfactory, considering the doom the God of the Jews has brought upon us. In a few short days, we will be free from His tyranny and step into our new age."

The King proceeded to repeat the same message in over fifty different languages! Every representative heard the message in his own language. The entire group stood for a screaming ovation as the King ended with, "Death to the God of the Jews!"

One by one, each representative filed past the King and shook his hand. They pushed everyone through at a rapid pace, allowing each one to introduce herself or himself and praise the King. The King nodded his head to each one and said, "Peace be to you."

My turn came and I stepped up to meet him. His blue eyes stared deep within my soul. I could feel his presence searching out my innermost thoughts. His warm smile never left his face, but I felt a cold chill rise up in my spine as he said, "Ahh, the United States official. I am ever so pleased to have you here. Your country has supported me from the beginning and I will not forget it. I do hope you write good things about me and the Great Victory."

"Umm. Yes, sir. You know I will," I stuttered nervously.

"Yes, I know you will," he replied in a deep, calm, and commanding voice while shaking my hand with both of his.

I looked down to the ground and stepped away. The image of his eyes pierced my heart. Even as I walked away, I felt the cold chill of what seemed to be his presence within my innermost being. He knew what I was thinking. He really knew.

The group sat back down and ate lunch after the King departed for the front line. Then we were told to rest in the hotel for the remainder of the night, and to get plenty of rest before the trip through the Plain of Esdraelon.

The Canadian official and I talked about the King for hours before we went to bed. He couldn't believe how the King actually spoke several sentences to me. I blew it off as no big deal, but deep down I felt quite proud of it. His words continued to echo in my mind. The warmth of his hands and the soothing smile are etched forever in my memory. This is a day I will never forget.

Day Six

We left this evening at seven for the trek through the valley. The group was transported by bus to a point three-fourths of the way down the valley. We were separated by fours and hopped on horses led by designated captains from the world army. I exchanged government addresses with my Canadian friend to get back in touch once we returned home. We waved to each other as the horses took us on our separate ways.

Torches and lanterns lined the narrow passageway through the waiting armies. Our group of five cantered down a narrow dirt roadway, weaving between the tens of thousands of troops marching to a closer position. Thousands upon thousands of soldiers stood along the roadside, creating a scene similar to that of people viewing a parade from the sidelines. Others played games and wandered around from tent to tent. Every now and then a caravan of honking jeeps and military vehicles drove by on their way to the front.

Around six a.m., our captain veered off the main roadway and slowed to a walk. We followed single file through the overcrowded campsites. The soldiers around us talked and laughed in an uncaring way. Their conversations centered around who would destroy the most angels and how they would do it. Each held their swords and guns, pretending to blast away into the air.

We rode into several foreign camps, dropping off the other officials with us, until we stopped at my destination. I stepped off my horse and was introduced to one of the field generals. One of his assistants took my belongings off the horse and put them into a tent next to the generals. After thanking the guide, I settled my stuff into my appointed tent, grateful for not having to share the space with anyone else. The assistant tapped on the canvas door, informing me that the general was awaiting my arrival.

Quickly, I combed my hair and put deodorant all over my body. I stepped out of the tent to see the smiling face of the assistant, who led me into the general's tent. The general greeted me and said, "We're pleased to have you be a part of our division in the Great Victory. Feel free to move around as you care to. Talk to the soldiers and ask them anything you like."

"Thank you, very much!" I replied.

We talked for about an hour on the support of the Americans and the unification of the world. I told him about the terrible condition of the country. Everyone's hope rested upon the King and the military forces gathered here. The support of the American people and the world was behind him.

With the King, he assured me, we were invincible. He related his stories about meeting the King and his experiences with him. The King was the most incredible, brilliant military strategist of all time in his mind. God would not dare try to actually remove the King with the support of the entire world behind him. He ended by shouting, "The Great Victory will soon be ours!"

I was so excited, I knocked the small glass of water off the table in front of us. "Oh, no, I'm so sorry," I apologized.

"That's okay. Soon we will have as much as we want," he said with a smile stretching from ear to ear.

He brought out one of his military maps and explained

our location in respect to the entire Great Victory forces. I questioned him about the best locations to visit to view the valley. He showed me the position of the King's camp and the closest point from which to see the Great Victory. We mapped out a path for me to follow and points along it to make sure I was on the right track. He warned me how difficult it is to maneuver through the valley in continual darkness; the lanterns seem to go on forever. I told him not to worry, I would be sure to check my position.

I walked to my tent, feeling the darkened sun break the night temperatures as it rose. The excitement of my journey prevented my falling asleep for an hour or so. In just a few days, I would be a part of the dawning of our new age.

Day Seven

The excitement of the soldiers is incredible! I talked to at least fifty different soldiers about their feelings and expectations. Not a single one regrets coming here, nor has anyone even expressed the slightest fear of defeat. Each one gladly responds to my questions without inhibition. They proudly display their symbol of the King and show complete trust in Him. Even I am amazed at the incredible amount of loyalty for the King and the willingness of everyone to talk about it.

One would think that the normal attitude of at least a few soldiers would be that of disagreement, or at least caution. Not here! Crowds would gather around me as I spoke to individuals, everyone loudly voicing their praise for the King and their excitement about the upcoming war with God. I even asked a group if they thought they were underestimating a worthy opponent such as God. They about tore my head off with screams of greatness for our god, our King. "We'll kick God's .... No one can beat our King. We'll blow him to ..." was the response of the entire crowd.

If the energy level at the other camps is the same, the King may have a hard time containing his troops! Whether it's hatred toward God for his plagues, or just loyalty toward our King, these soldiers are ready to fight!

Day Eight

I'm at my first stop on my journey toward my viewing spot. It's a British camp with very helpful officers. They gave me cold blood to drink and took care of my horse. I'm sitting in one of the few remaining tents with a portable fan blowing on my face. I asked one of the officers why the tents were being taken down. He replied, "The King expects the Great Victory to begin as early as tomorrow. He ordered all troops to prepare for battle. After all divisions are ready, we will move even closer toward the front so others back toward the end of the valley can fit in."

He just informed me I needed to hurry before the paths for my horse would be cut off by the advancing troops. I'll write more at my next break.

• • • • •

I'm at another American division, sitting on the ground next to my horse. Soldiers crowd around me picking up the remains of their camp. One of the officers here gave me another map with a little different route to follow. He said the main road I intended to gallop down was already crowded over with troops. My only chance of passage to my viewing spot was another specially blocked-off road for the King's vehicles. He said with my special pass, I should have no problem getting through.

The route's going to take longer, so I have to cut my break short.

• • • • •

I just reached the last stop before my destination. I'm at an Australian division, with about a mile left to go. The officers are taking good care of me and my horse. They are loading up enough supplies to last a few days, as I will' not have a chance to replenish them again until after the Great Victory. Some soldiers also gave me some newly developed bird repellent spray to ward off the birds from my food. I can't believe how many birds are gathered in the valley. They fly around our heads and sometimes are quite aggressive for food.

On this last stretch, I used the King's road for about three miles and was stopped twice by military police. After I showed my special pass, they wished me well and apologized for the inconvenience. Once off the King's road, movement became slow and tedious as throngs of soldiers blocked the path and the light from the road dimmed behind me. My horse bumped and pushed its way through the people crowded around us. No one seemed to want to give way to those crossing.

I have about two hours to reach my final destination and beat the rise in temperature. One of the Australian officers gave me a horn to sound every so often to warn those in front to get out of the way. He figures it should take less than an hour to get across the final mile.

The only other major obstacle is the increase in heavy machinery down here. The closer to the front I come, the bigger and more abundant the firepower becomes. I'm beginning to see tanks as well as more cannon and even missiles. One of the officers explained, "The missiles and heavy artillery are concentrated on the front and sides of the valley, rather than in the middle. It gives more protection and safety to those it surrounds."

My horse is ready. I'll finish when I arrive at my viewing point.

• • • • •

I just finished laying out my sheet beneath a missile launcher! The control man for the section of missiles I'm in, assured me he would sound a warning before he fired. Still, it's a little nerve-wracking to be underneath this metal cylinder full of explosives.

Ten feet from my sheet is one of the rocks at the edge of the Valley of Esdraelon. I will begin the ascent to my viewing point from here. The control man said to move at least five hundred feet from the missiles to be safe, and about one thousand feet to be comfortable. I'll make sure to be at least a thousand feet away!

The observation that stuck in my mind the most, was the many nationalities meshing together. As I rode through the millions of troops, the unity of Blacks, Whites, Orientals, and every nationality on earth blended into one fighting force. I can still picture in my mind when I passed between a Japanese unit and a French unit. Though all were dressed in their respective national uniforms, they walked side by side and intermixed toward their goal. Instead of looking to the sides and fighting with each other, they looked only ahead to the task at hand. Our King has successfully united us into fighting for our planet. We don't want God to rule over us with his tyranny. We want our King, who has done so much for the good of our planet, to be our God.

Day Nine

I'm finally here, sitting above the plain, ready to observe the Great Victory. I have my binoculars, plenty of paper, several pens, a flat rock to sit on, blood to drink, and a little corn to eat. This event will be the highlight of my life... everyone's life! What an awesome opportunity.

Trying to get up here was quite a chore. I had to chase birds away from every spot I crawled to. They pecked at my hands, feet, head, and especially the food. Several times, I almost fell into crevices after slipping on the bird dung. Now that I have settled in a spot, the birds just fly all around me or sit down next to me. The only time they become aggressive is when I take a drink of blood, at which time I use the repellent spray the soldiers gave me.

The rock I'm sitting on and the entire hill surrounding the valley is only fifty feet high. The great earthquake wiped out the majestic hills and mountains and left this pile of rocks around the valley. Still, the view of the valley and all the troops is incredible. As far as I can see with my binoculars are the little lights from all the torches and lanterns. It reminds me of sitting by the Hollywood sign in California and looking out over the city. Except this time, there is no end to the people or lights. For miles upon miles the valley is filled with hundreds of millions of troops. All ready to fight for their planet. It is the greatest fighting force ever established in the history of the world. Every nation on earth represented by tens of millions of troops. All led by the King!

• • • • •

It's been almost five hours since I first made it to this rock. No one knows when the battle will commence. Our King will attack the Jews as soon as he feels everyone is in place. It shouldn't take longer than a day or two to begin the offensive, and hopefully not very much longer in finishing because my supplies will only last two more days.

As I gaze over the massive army poised to strike, the past seven years have flashed back through my mind. My wife laughing and talking about our plans together. Wrestling with the kids. The deaths. The pain and suffering. The resurrection of our King. The loss of our children. The loss of my wife. The emptiness. The hope.

Many ideas have crossed my mind on what I will do when I go home. Starting my own company seems to be the logical and exciting thing to do. Before that, I think I'll take a vacation down to Hawaii… assuming, of course, that the oceans become clean again, as our King promised. Hawaii might be a good place to start a company. Working for the government a little longer wouldn't be too bad either. The pay and benefits would allow me to rebuild and establish myself once again. Another possibility I have tossed around is actually coming to work for the King in some capacity. The chance seems small of landing a position, but it would be worth a try!

• • • • •

A helicopter shone its light upon me a few moments ago. I flashed my pass toward them and it continued on searching the hills. It stops every few hundred yards or so with its light shining on military posts. The closest one to me is about four hundred yards to the south. With binoculars, I can see the glow of the sentry's flashlight. For some reason, none of the posts on the hillside are using torches or fires, possibly due to not wanting an identifiable mark of their position.

• • • • •

In the last hour or so, there has been an abundance of jets and helicopters flying overhead. They announced over my English short-wave radio that the King wants the first assault on the Jews to begin precisely at midnight, only moments away. From the plans they discussed with all the country representatives, the first assault would be with air-to-ground missiles.

The few lights remaining on the hillside just went out. I can hear the jets coming! The roar from the jets is incredible. There have to be thousands of fighters above us. I can see the first missiles being shot.

Wait. The clouds are opening up above the valley and light is pouring down. No, it can't be! My eyes can barely see through the blinding brightness of light. A magnificent white horse is descending from the skies with someone on its back! How can this happen? Oh, my God, it's Jesus Christ! No! It's not possible. His brightness is too much! I can't … I can't … I can't ….

The Day After

"There was a certain rich man, which was clothed in purple and fine linen, and fared sumptuously, every day: And there was a certain beggar named Lazarus, which was laid at his gate, full of sores, And desiring to be fed with the crumbs which fell from the rich man's table: moreover the dogs came and licked his sores. And it came to pass, that the beggar died, and was carried by the angels into Abraham's bosom: the rich man also died, and was buried; And in hell he lifted up his eyes, being in torments, and seeth Abraham afar off and Lazarus in his bosom. And he cried and said. Father Abraham, have mercy on me, and send Lazarus, that he may dip the tip of his finger in water, and cool my tongue, for I am tormented in this flame. But Abraham said, Son, remember that thou in thy lifetime receivedst thy good things, and likewise Lazarus evil things: but now he is comforted, and thou art tormented. And beside all this, between us and you there is a great gulf fixed: so that they which would pass from hence to you cannot; neither can they pass to us, that would come from thence. Then he said, I pray thee therefore, father, that thou wouldst send him to my father's house: For I have five brethren; that he may testify unto them, lest they also come into this place of torment. Abraham saith unto him, They have Moses and the prophets; let them hear them. And he said, Nay, father Abraham: but if one went unto them from the dead, they will repent. And he said unto him, If they hear not Moses and the prophets, neither will they be persuaded, though one rose from the dead" (Luke 16:19-31).

"And I saw the dead, small and great, stand before God; and the books were opened; and another book was opened,

which is the book of life: and the dead were judged out of those things which were written in the books, according to their works. And the sea gave up the dead which were in it; and death and hell delivered up the dead which were in them: and they were judged every man according to their works. And death and hell were cast into the lake of fire. This is the second death. And whosoever was not found written in the book of life was cast into the lake of fire" (Rev. 20:12-15).

Epilogue

Unfortunately, the story you just read does not end. On the contrary, it is only the beginning. In Revelation 19:20-21, the Bible clearly states that anyone who receives the mark would be killed at the battle of Armageddon. Then, each person would descend into Hell. In Luke 16:19-31, Jesus explained what it was like to be in Hell. The pain and agony was so great that one drop of water could relieve just a bit of the torture, but it was impossible to get that one drop. As horrible as the Tribulation will be here on earth when God's wrath is poured out, it is nothing compared to an eternity separated from the Lord in a burning torment. Even now, people are screaming from Hell, begging you not to come down where they are (Luke 16:27-31). The Lord ***does not want you to perish away from Him! God wants you to be in Heaven with Him when you die?*** (2 Pet. 3:9).

Unfortunately, your sins have separated you from the Most Holy God (Isa. 59:2). You are *not worthy* to be in Heaven with a perfect God (Rom. 3:23). The price to be paid for sinning against God is an eternal death apart from Him in eternal torment (Rom. 6:23). But, ***God loves you so much*** that He decided to pay the price for you to go to Heaven. God sent His only Son, Jesus Christ, to live a perfect and holy life on earth. Jesus was the ***only one*** who deserved to enter Heaven, because He was perfect. Instead, He allowed people to beat Him, curse Him, and crucify Him, that through His death, *you* could have life (Isa. 53:5-6; John 3: 16; 6:47; 14:6; Rom. 6:23; I John 3: 14; 5:1 l; John 20:31, and so many more)! ***The one way to Heaven is through Jesus Christ the Lord?***

Reading on through Revelation 20-22, the two types of afterlife are explained. In Revelation 20:11-15, everyone whose name is not written in the Book of Life is cast into an eternal death in the lake of fire, always to be tormented and separated from the righteous and holy God. In Revelation 21-22, God tells us of the many blessings and eternal life in store for those who are written in the Book of Life. Whose names are written in the Book of Life? Only those who have trusted in Jesus Christ as their *own personal Savior!* There is no in-between: it's either eternal life and the many blessings, or eternal death and the torment.

God loves you. He does not want you to be separated from Him. He sent Jesus Christ to carry out *your* death sentence, so that *you* could have eternal life. Jesus wants you to be with Him for eternity. He paid the price and is offering the *gift* of eternal life to you right now! Will you turn Him away and face the wrath of God (Rom. 5:9)? Or will you take the gift of eternal life from Jesus Christ (Eph. 2:8-9)? You must make the decision *now!* To wait until later is to deny Him, and you may not get a second chance. The choice is yours.

• • • • •

For further information or questions about eternal life, *please* write to:

Brad Keating
C/O Bible Truth
P.O. Box 8550
Wichita, KS 67208

Audio cassettes of the series "From Now to Eternity" are also available.

References By Chapters

Day One

1 Thessalonians 4:13-5:7; Revelation 4:1,2; 1 Corinthians 15:51-53; Genesis 5:24; 2 Peter 3:1-9; Luke 12:37-40; Matthew 24:36-42; Daniel 9:27; John 14:1-3; 2 Thessalonians 2:3-12

Week One

Revelation 6:1-2; Mark 13:6; Matthew 24:5

Year One

Revelation 6:3-4; Mark 13:7-8; Matthew 24:6; Luke 21:10; Ezekiel 38-39; Daniel 2:40-43; 7:7-8,23-24

One Year, Six Months

Revelation 6:5-6; Matthew 24:7; Mark 13:8; Luke 21:11; Ezekiel 36:29-30

Two Years

Revelation 6:7-8; Luke 21:11; Matthew 24:7; Mark 13:8

Two Years, Six Months

Revelation 6:9-11; 13:1-10; 17:1-11; Daniel 7:8, 23-28; 8:23-27; 11:36-45; 2 Thessalonians 2; 9-12

Three Years

Revelation 6:12-17; Matthew 24:7; Mark 13:8; Luke 21:11

Three Years, Six Months

Revelation 13:11-14; 17:8-11

Three Days Later

Revelation 13:11-14; 17:8-11

Eight Days Later

Revelation 8:7; Daniel 12:1; Matthew 24:21-22; Mark 13:19-20

Three Years, Seven Months

Revelation 13:11-18; 17:12-17

The Next Day

Revelation 13:11-18; 17:12-17

Three Years, Eight Months

Revelation 13:11-18; 17:12-17

Three Years, Nine Months

Revelation 8:8-9; Daniel 7:25

Four Years, Six Months

Revelation 8:10-13

Four Years, Ten Months

Revelation 9:1-12

Five Years

Revelation 9:13-21; 2 Timothy 3:4-5

Five Years, Four Months

Revelation 16:3-7

Five Years, Eleven Months

No specific references

Six Years, Four Months

Revelation 16:8-11

Six Years, Nine Months

Revelation 16:12-21

Six Years, Ten Months

No specific references

Six Years, Ten Months, Two Weeks

Revelation 14:14-20; 19:11-21; Ezekiel 39:17-21

How Prophecies Affect Your Future

In studying the return of Christ, we find that three important issues stand out from all others: Israel becoming a nation, at least sixty prophecies fulfilled for the Lord's return to earth, and the seventh day of rest. Any one of these three is in itself enough to point to Christ's soon return, but all three together can lead to only one conclusion: the trumpet is about to blow!

Israel Becomes a Nation (1948)

The one prophecy that had to be fulfilled was for Israel to be re-established as a nation. There are so many references to Israel's return from among the Gentile nations that no other prophecies would make sense until it happened.

Daniel 9:27 depicts the Antichrist signing a peace treaty with Israel for seven years (giving us the length of the Tribulation), but how can he sign a peace treaty with a country that doesn't exist? The logical conclusion is that the Tribulation could not begin until Israel, as a nation, could sign a peace treaty. Ezekiel 36-39 depict Israel's return to war against Russia and her allies. In Ezekiel 37:15-28, God goes a step farther to predict Israel coming back as one nation, not the two nations of Israel and Judah. Miraculously, after Hitler tried to totally wipe out all Jews from the planet, they were united as one nation and given back a portion of their old land in 1948.

Jesus made predictions about Israel and Jerusalem. In Matthew 24:2, He predicted the destruction of the temple and how it would be done. He went on in Matthew 24:3-31 to explain the Tribulation and the signs accompanying his return. Then in verse 32, He predicts Israel's return as a nation, but without fruit. Today, Israel is a prominent nation in the Middle East, but there is no spiritual return to the Lord. In verse 33, Jesus warned that when you see Israel bud and grow as a tender nation, the Tribulation is very near. In verse 34, He takes it a step farther and says that the generation that sees Israel bud and become a nation would not die until they saw Jesus' return. How long this generation is, no one knows, but one fact is sure: The greatest majority of those that witnessed Israel's return as a nation would also witness Christ's return!

Many Prophecies Fulfilled Since Israel Became a Nation

I have found at least sixty prophecies that have been fulfilled in the last few decades for the Tribulation and the Day of the Lord (thousand-year reign of Christ on earth). Others claim even more. There are a few that seem a bit farfetched, but most are quite obvious. One cannot deny the evidence of so many prophecies being fulfilled in such a short time period since Israel's return as a nation.

To further explain how one can rely on these as accurate, let me take a few examples (it would take an entire book to do all of them). Revelation 11:8-9, clearly depicts the entire world viewing the two bodies that lie dead in Jerusalem. Since it would be physically impossible for the entire world population to fly to Jerusalem within three and a half days to actually look at the bodies, God would have to bring about something to fulfill this prophecy. Low and behold, in the 1950s (after Israel was a nation), satellites were sent up into space. Today, the entire world can view the happenings in Israel in a matter of seconds. The prophecy of Revelation 11 can now be fulfilled! In Revelation 19:17 and Ezekiel 39:17-20, God calls for birds to gather in Megiddo to eat the flesh that will be destroyed in the battle of Armageddon. Just in the last few years, millions of birds have used that area as nesting grounds and a point of stopping between Europe and Africa. Coincidence? Don't count on it!

Still in doubt? How about the graphic depiction of the effects of a neutron bomb in Zechariah 14:12? God describes a plague in the last days that melts the flesh off the bones, melts the eyes out of their sockets and the tongue in the mouth, all while the person is actually standing! As gross as this is, God knew and predicted exactly what happens when a neutron bomb is exploded. Unlike a normal nuclear explosion, which fuses and disintegrates everything around it, a neutron bomb destroys only living matter and leaves buildings and tanks unharmed. Coincidence?. Not a chance. God said that in the last days, these powers would be found and used.

Even if a few seem to be hard to accept, the greatest majority of the sixty prophecies are graphic and accurate. All have been fulfilled since Israel became a nation. One cannot deny the inescapable fact that these prophecies are paving the way for the very soon return of the Lord Jesus Christ!

The Seventh Day of Rest

Of the three main issues I faced in studying the return of Jesus Christ, this was the hardest to understand and the most convincing of all as to how soon Jesus Christ would be returning to reign a thousand years on earth. Alone, this prophecy would have a hard time holding water as to its significance, but with the two previous issues discussed, it stands out as the one that ties everything together and manifests itself in a sobering reality of how little time is left.

The main prophetic passage to be used is 2 Peter 3:3-13. Upon reading these eleven verses dealing with the second coming of Jesus Christ, verse 8 sticks out like a sore thumb. *"But beloved, be not* ***ignorant*** *of this* ***one*** *thing, that one day is with the Lord as a thousand years, and a thousand years as one day."* Why, in the middle of eleven prophetic verses, would the Lord warn us not to be ignorant of one thing, if it weren't prophetic? It would not make sense to be talking about the return of His own Son, stop for one verse and warn us not to be ignorant of *one* fact, then continue on with more about the second coming, if the *one* fact did not pertain to the prophetic passage! We can easily conclude that the *one* thing Verse 8 is speaking of is the return of Christ, just like all the others around it. So what does this verse mean?

The main aspect of the verse equates one day with a thousand years. Are there any other passages in the Bible that equate a day with a thousand years? There surely are. Throughout the writings of the Old Testament prophets, the term "the day of the Lord" is used in connection with judgment to the Gentile nations, as well as the glorification of Jerusalem and Israel. This is a period of time that extends longer than our twenty-four-hour "day," and it will be a time of rest for Israel and the world. The time frame of one thousand years is given in Revelation 20:1-7, when Christ will reign upon earth in Jerusalem and Satan will be restrained from interfering with planetary peace. It is promised by God that the one thousand years will be a time of rest for the nations as Jesus Christ reigns as earthly ruler and lifts the curse off the ground. In God's eyes, this thousand-year period is just one day in His time frame. Does this really have anything to do with being prophetic? YES!

Without going into much detail (one could write an entire book just on this subject), Adam was created approximately in 4000 B.C., give or take a year or two. We are quickly approaching the year A.D. 2000, which happens to be six thousand years since the beginning of creation. In God's eyes, we are about to complete the sixth day. In Genesis 2:2-3, what did God do on the seventh day? In the Mosaic law, what did God command to do on the seventh day? God also took the people out of Israel and into Babylon for seventy years to give the land rest because the nation had not been observing the Sabbath. The seventh day is a day of *rest.* When Christ reigns for one thousand years, the nations and earth will be at *rest.*

Remember, the thousand-year reign of Christ could *not* take place until Israel became a nation once again. Isn't it amazing how Israel became a nation just in time for the seventh day?

Do not forget that quite a few prophecies need to be fulfilled before the thousand-year reign of Christ could begin. If we are to believe that around the year A.D. 2000, Christ would begin his reign, then logically we can assume many prophecies would be fulfilled in the years just prior to A.D. 2000. Isn't it amazing how at least sixty prophecies have been fulfilled since Israel became a nation and just in time for the seventh day?

Jesus Christ *never* said we would not know the general time of His return. On the contrary, He told us the signs of His return and said that when we saw them, we would *know* He was right at the door. He told us only we could not know the day or hour.

Still not convinced? There's more.

Another prominent passage is Hosea 5:14-6:2. In speaking to the Jews, God identifies Himself as having come and returning to His own place (vs. 14-15). He warns of their destruction and how He would take their nation away. In Hosea 6:1-2, Israel declares how God had punished them, and that through Him they can live again. Verse 2 explains how Israel would be dead for two days and be revived to live on the third day. The third day is further identified as living in the *sight* of God.

Jesus Christ arrived either in the year 1 B.C. Or A.D. 1, depending upon which book one reads (there is no year A.D. 0). It just happens to be that the year A.D. 2000 will be two days since God came to the Jews. As explained before, for one thousand years (or one day) Jesus will reign in Israel over the entire earth. All of Israel will be living in His sight! Is it coincidence that for almost two days Israel ceased to exist and has been revived just prior to the third day? Is it coincidence that this third day of living in the *sight* of God parallels perfectly with the seventh day of rest? Do God's plans ever happen by coincidence, or are they specifically set out with a purpose?

As I studied these and many other prophecies of Christ's return, it became apparent that our time is very short. We cannot count on the year A.D. 2000 being the exact year for the beginning of the one thousand years, because some place the time of Adam's creation as early as 4002 B.C. Our calendars are not as accurate as the Lord's. Even if one wants to hope to have a few years before A.D. 2000 or so, think again. Before the thousand year reign, there needs to be a seven-year Tribulation first! Though we cannot set an exact date for our Lord's return, anyone can see the time is *now!*

If you are lucky enough to read this before the Rapture occurs, I hope you have already made the decision to accept Jesus Christ as your personal Messiah.

If you haven't, why not do it right now? Confess to the Lord that you are a sinner (Rom. 3:23). Realize that the punishment for these sins is eternal death in the lake of fire (Rom. 6:23). Then accept what Jesus Christ did on the cross as *a free gift* (Rom. 6:23), in place of the penalty that you should have paid. All it really means is that you will *trust* in Jesus Christ to take you into Heaven, rather than depending upon *anything* that you could possibly do (Eph. 2:8-9). Jesus offers you eternal life because He loved *you* enough to pay the penalty for your sin. Will you accept Him as your Savior, or go into the Tribulation period and then die an eternal death in the lake of fire? The payment is made. The gift is offered. The choice is yours.

For further information on eternal life, Hell, the Tribulation, *how you* can be saved, or any other questions regarding the Bible, *please* write to:

Brad Keating
C/O Bible Truth
P.O. Box 8550
Wichita, KS 67208

Bible Prophecies Fulfilled

1.	1930s	Evolution accepted instead of creation (2 Pet. 3:3-7)
2.	1940	World War 1I- the *entire* world at war (Matt. 24:7)
3.	1945	Nuclear weapon (2 Pet. 3:10)
4.	1948	Israel becomes a nation (Matt. 24:32-36; Zech. 14; Ezek. 36,37 and many more)
5.	1948	Israel as one nation (not two) (Ezek. 37:15-28)
6.	1948	Iran opposes Israel (Ezek. 38:4-6)
7.	1948	Iraq opposes Israel (Ezel. 38:4-6)
8.	1950s	Rainy season twice a year (Hos. 6:3; Joel 2:23)
9.	1950s	Russia opposes Israel (Ezek. 38-39)
10.	1950s	Russia becomes a world power (Ezek. 38-39)
11.	1950s	Turkey allies with Russia and opposes Israel (Ezek. 38:4-6)
12.	1950s	Satellite television (Rev. 11:8-9)
13.	1950s	Military rockets are gas powered (Nah. 2:3-4)
14.	1960s	Widespread air travel (Dan. 12:4; Amos 8:12)
15.	1960s	Computers (Dan. 12:4; Rev. 13:16-17)
16.	1960s	Neutron bomb (Zech. 14:12)
17.	1973	Golan Heights becomes a part of Israel (Jer. 50:19)
18.	1973	Carmel becomes part of Israel (Jer. 50:19)
19.	1973	Jerusalem becomes part of Israel (Zech. 14:12)

20. 1970s	"Me first" attitude (2 Tim. 3:1-5)
21. 1984	Oil found in Israel at the foot of Asher (Deut. 33:24)
22. 1984	Oil wells and rigs in Asher (Deut. 33:25)
23. 1986	Libya allies with Russia and opposes Israel (Ezek. 38:4-6)
24. 1988	Ethiopia allies with Russia and opposes Israel (Ezek. 38:4-6)
25. 1988	1ran and Iraq make peace (Ezek. 38:4-6)
26. 1989	Canal built between the Mediterranean and Dead Sea (Ezek. 47:6-8)
27. 1980s	Roses blossom in Israel (Isa. 35:1)
28. 1980s	Israel fills the world with produce (Isa.27:6)
29. 1980s	Israel has up to seven harvests a year (Amos 9:13)
30. 1980s	Barren wasteland becomes fruitful (Ezek. 36:35)
31. 1980s	Hebrew becomes the official language (Zeph. 3:9)
32. 1980s	The shekel becomes the monetary system (Ezek. 45:12)
33. 1980s	Jericho built from refuse (Amos 9:13-14; Ezek. 36:35)
34. 1980s	Nazareth built from refuse (Amos 9: 13-14; Ezek. 36:35)
35. 1980s	Ashkelon rebuilt (Zeph. 2:4;Amos 9:I3-14; Ezek. 36:35)
36. 1980s	Ashdod rebuilt (Zeph. 2:4; Amos 9:13-14; Ezek. 36:35)
37. 1980s	Egypt allies with Russia and opposes Israel (Ezek. 38:4-6)
38. 1980s	U.S. questions Russia and backs Israel (Ezek. 38:13)
39. 1980s	England questions Russia and backs Israel (Ezek. 38:13)

40.	1980s	Canada questions Russia and backs Israel (Ezek. 38:13)
41.	1980s	Churches seek pleasure and money (2Tim. 3:4-6)
42.	1980s	Earthquakes (Matt. 24:7)
43.	1980s	Famines worldwide (Matt. 24:7)
44.	1980s	Pestilences: AIDS, cancer, venereal diseases, etc. (Matt. 24:7)
45.	1990	Germany united (Ezek. 38:6)
46.	1991	Many nations oppose Iraq (old Babylon) (Jer. 50:9,41)
47.	1991	Missiles will be perfectly shot (Jer. 50:9)
48.	1991	Hussein becomes afraid (Jer. 50:43)
49.	1991	Iraq's elite guard refuses to fight (Jer. 51: 30)
50.	1991	All nations hear of Iraq's fall (Jer. 50:46)
51.	1991	Iraq filled with men shouting against it (Jer. 51:14)
52.	1991	Foreign troops in Middle East (Isa. 13:4-5; Rev. 19)
53.	1990s	Jews flee from Russia to Israel (Zech. 2:6)
54.	1990s	Jews flock back to their homeland (Ezek. 36,37; Zech. 14; Amos, and many others)
55.	1990s	Different wars all over the world (Matt. 24:7)
56.	1990s	World dependent on Middle East for oil (Jer. 51:7)
57.	1990s	Debit cards (Rev. 13:16-17)
58.	1990s	Scoffers at second coming of Jesus Christ (2 Pet. 3:3)
59.	1990s	Many claim to be "Christ" (Matt. 24:5)
60.	Present	Israel a world power with a great army (Ezek. 37:10)
61.	Present	Israel has not, nor will have, a famine (Ezek. 36:29-30)

62.	Present	Israel will never be destroyed again (Matt. 24:32-36; Zech. 14; Ezek. 36-37 and many others)
63.	Present	Many fowl(birds) gather in Megiddo (Rev. 19:17; Ezek. 39:17-20)
64.	Present	Pause in time before the final elimination (Jer. 51:33)
65.	Present	Forming of ten nations in Europe (Dan. 2:26-45; 7:1-28: Rev. 13:1; 17:1-18)
66.	Present	One-world government (Daniel and Revelation)
67.	Present	One-world bank (Rev. 13:16-17)
68.	Present	One-world religion (Rev. 17)
69.	Present	Peace Treaty with PLO, Sept. 13, 1993 (Daniel 9:27)